T

Edgar Wallace was born illegitimately in 1875 in Greenwich and adopted by George Freeman, a porter at Billingsgate fish market. At eleven, Wallace sold newspapers at Ludgate Circus and on leaving school took a job with a printer. He enlisted in the Royal West Kent Regiment, later transferring to the Medical Staff Corps, and was sent to South Africa. In 1898 he published a collection of poems called

To renew this book take it to any of
the City Libraries before
the date due for return

Coventry City Council

BY THE SAME AUTHOR
ALL PUBLISHED BY HOUSE OF STRATUS

The Clue of the
Silver Key

HOUSE OF
STRATUS

This edition published in 2001 by House of Stratus, an imprint of
Stratus Books Ltd., 21 Beeching Park, Kelly Bray,
Cornwall, PL17 8QS, UK.
www.houseofstratus.com

Typeset, printed and bound by House of Stratus.

A catalogue record for this book is available from the British Library
and the Library of Congress.

ISBN 1-84232-667-8

We would like to thank the Edgar Wallace Society for all the support they have given
House of Stratus. Enquiries on how to join the Edgar Wallace Society should be addressed to:
The Edgar Wallace Society, c/o Penny Wyrd, 84 Ridgefield Road, Oxford, OX4 3DA.
Email: info@edgarwallace.org Web: http://www.edgarwallace.org/

DEDICATED TO MICHAEL BEARY

1

They were all in this business – Dick Allenby, inventor and heir-at-law; Jerry Dornford, man about town and wastrel; Mike Hennessey, theatrical adventurer; Mary Lane, small part actress; Leo Moran, banker and speculator; Horace Tom Tickler (alas, for him!) was very much in it, though he knew nothing about it.

Mr Washington Wirth, who gave parties and loved flattery; old Hervey Lyne and the patient Binny, who pulled his bath-chair and made his breakfast and wrote his letters – and Surefoot Smith.

There came a day when Binny, who was an assiduous reader of newspapers that dealt with the more picturesque aspects of crime, was to find himself the focal point of attention and his evidence read by millions who had never before heard of him – a wonderful experience.

Mr Washington Wirth's parties were most exclusive affairs and, in a sense, select. The guests were chosen with care, and might not, in the manner of the age, invite the uninvited to accompany them; but they were, as Mary Lane said, "an odd lot." She went because Mike Hennessey asked her, and she rather liked the stout and lethargic Mike. People called him "poor old Mike" because of his bankruptcies, but just now sympathy would be wasted on him. He had found Mr Washington Wirth, a patron of the theatre and things theatrical, and Mr Washington Wirth was a very rich man.

He was also a mysterious man. He was generally believed to live in the Midlands and to be associated with industry. His London address was the Kellner Hotel, but he never slept there. His secretary would telephone in advance for the Imperial suite on a certain day, and on the evening of that day, when supper was laid for his twenty or thirty guests, and the specially hired orchestra was tuning up, he would appear, a stout, flaxen-haired man in horn-rimmed spectacles. The uncharitable said his flaxen hair was a wig, which may or may not have been true.

He was perfectly tailored, invariably wore white kid gloves. He spoke in a high, falsetto voice, had a trick of clicking his heels and kissing the hands of his lady guests which was very Continental.

His guests were hand-picked. He chose – or Mike chose for him – the smaller theatrical fry; chorus girls, small part ladies, an obscure singer or two.

Once Mike had suggested a brighter kind of party. Mr Wirth was shocked.

"I want nothing fast," he said.

He loved adulation – and had his fill of it. He was a generous spender, a giver of expensive presents; people living on the verge of poverty might be excused a little flattering.

You could not gate-crash into one of Mr Washington Wirth's parties, invitations to which came in the shape of a small oblong badge, not unlike the badge worn by the ladies in the Royal Enclosure at Ascot, on which the name of the invited guest was written. This the recipient wore; it served a double purpose, for it enabled Mr Wirth to read and address each of his guests by her name.

Mary Lane was well aware that the invitation was no tribute to her own eminence.

"I suppose if I had been a really important guest I shouldn't have been invited?" she said.

Mike smiled good-naturedly.

"You *are* important, Mary – the most important person here, my dear. The old boy was keen to know you."

"Who is he?"

Mike shook his head.

"He's got all the money in the world," he said.

She laughed. Mary Lane was very lovely when she laughed. She was conscious that Washington Wirth, albeit occupied with the cooing attention of two blonde lovelies, was watching her out of the side of his eyes.

"He gives lots of parties, doesn't he?" she asked. "Mr Allenby told me today that they are monthly affairs. He must be rich, of course, or he wouldn't keep our play running. Honestly, Mike, we must be losing a fortune at the Sheridan."

Mike Hennessey took his cigar from his mouth and looked at the ash.

"I'm not losing a fortune," he said. Then, most unexpectedly: "Old Hervey Lyne a friend of yours, Mary?"

She denied the friendship with some vigour.

"No, he's my guardian. Why?"

Mike put back his cigar deliberately.

The band had struck up a waltz. Mr Wirth was gyrating awkwardly, holding at arm's length a lady from the Jollity who was used to being held more tightly.

"I had an idea you were connected," he said. "Moneylender, wasn't he? That's how he made his stuff. Is Mr Allenby related to him?"

There was a certain significance in the question, and she flushed.

"Yes – his nephew." She was a little disconcerted. "Why?"

Mike looked past her at the dancers.

"Trying to pretend they enjoy it," he said. "They're all getting gold-mounted vanity bags tonight – you'll get yours."

"But why do you ask about Mr Lyne?" she persisted.

"Just wondering how well you knew the old man. No, he's never lent me money. He wants gilt-edged security and I've never had it. Moran's his banker."

Mike was one of those disconcerting men whose speech followed the eccentric course of their thoughts.

He chuckled.

"Funny, that, Mary. Moran's his banker. You don't see the joke, but I do."

She knew Leo Moran slightly. He was by way of being a friend of Dick Allenby's, and he was, she knew, a frequent visitor to the theatre, though he never came "back stage."

3

When Mike was being cryptic it was a waste of time trying to catch up with him. She looked at her watch.

"Will he be very annoyed if I leave soon? I have promised to go on to the Legation."

He shook his head, took her gently by the arm, and led her up to where Mr Wirth was being delightfully entertained by three pretty girls who were trying to guess his age.

"My little friend has to go, Mr Wirth," he said. "She's got a rehearsal in the morning."

"Perfectly understood!" said the host.

When he smiled he had white, even teeth, for which no thanks were due to nature.

"Per-fectly understood. Come again, Miss Mary Lane. I'll be back from abroad in three weeks."

She took his big, limp hand and shook it. Mike escorted her out and helped her into her coat.

"Another hour for me and then I pack up," he said. "He never stays after one. By the way, I'll bring on your gift to the theatre."

She liked Mike – everybody liked Mike. There was hardly an actor or an actress in London who had not agreed to take half-salary from him. He could cry very convincingly when he was ruined, and he was always ruined when hard-hearted people expected him to pay what he owed them.

A lovable soul, entirely dishonest. Nobody knew what he did with the money which he had lost for so many people, but the probability is that it was usefully employed.

"I don't know what's the matter with our play," he said, as he walked with her along the corridor to the elevator. "Maybe it's the title – *Cliffs of Fate* – what does it mean? I've seen the darn' thing forty times and still I don't know what it's about."

She stared at him, aghast.

"But you chose it!" she protested.

He shook his head.

"He did." He jerked his thumb back to Mr Wirth's suite. "He said it made him feel a better man when he read it. It's never made me want to go more regularly to the synagogue!"

He saw Mary depart, fussed over her like a broody hen. He liked Mary because she was real in a world of unreality. The first time he had taken her out to supper he had offered her a few suggestions on the quickest method by which a young actress might reach stardom, and her name in lights, and she had answered him sanely and yet in a way that did not entirely wound his vanity – and the vanity of a fat man is prodigious.

Thereafter she went into a new category: he had many; she was the only woman in the world he really liked, though, it is said, he loved many. He strolled back to the hectic atmosphere of the supper-room – Mr Wirth was presenting the bags.

He was unusually gay: usually he drank very little, but tonight… Well, he had promised to drink a whole bottle of champagne if anybody guessed his age, and one of the three pretty girls had guessed thirty-two.

"Good God!" said Mike, when they told him.

As soon as was expedient he took his patron aside.

"About time these people went, Mr Wirth," he said.

Mr Wirth smiled foolishly; spoke with the refeenment which wine brings to some.

"My deah, deah fellah! I'm quate ceepable of draving myself to deah old Coventry."

Certainly this was a new Mr Wirth. Mike Hennessey was troubled. He felt he was in danger of losing a priceless possession. It was as though the owner of a secret gold mine, from which he was drawing a rich dividend, were hoisting a great flapping flag to mark its site.

"What you want," he said agitatedly, "is something cooling. Just wait here, will you?"

He ran out, saw the head waiter, and came back very soon with a little blue bottle. He measured a tablespoonful of white granules into a wine-glass and filled it with water; then he handed this fizzling, hissing potion to the giver of the feast.

"Drink," he said.

Mr Wirth obeyed. He stopped and gasped between the gulps.

By now the last guest had gone.

"All right?" asked Mike anxiously.

"Quite all right," snapped the other.

He seemed suddenly sober. Mike, at any rate, was deceived. He did not see his friend to his car because that was against the rules. Mr Wirth, wrapped in a heavy coat, the collar of which was turned up, his opera hat at a rakish angle over his eyes, made his way to the garage near the hotel, had his car brought out, and was getting into it when the watcher sidled up to him.

"Can I have a word with you, mister?"

Mr Wirth surveyed him glassily, climbed into his seat and shifted his gear.

"Can I have a word – "

The car jerked forward. The little interviewer, who had one foot on the running board, was sent sprawling. He got up and began to run after the car, to the amusement of the garage workers; car and pursuer vanished in the darkness.

6

2

The trailer lost his quarry in Oxford Street and wandered disconsolately onward. A sort of homing instinct led him towards Regent's Park. Naylors Crescent was a magnificent little side street leading from the outer circle. It was very silent, its small, but stately, houses were in darkness.

Mr Tickler – such was his peculiar name – stopped before No. 17 and looked up at the windows. The white blinds were drawn down and the house was lifeless. He stood, with his hands thrust into his pockets, blinking at the green door that he knew so well, at the three worn steps leading down, and the hollow steel railway that masons had fixed into the stonework to allow the easy descent of a bath-chair.

Inside was wealth, immense, incalculable wealth, and a stupid old man on the verge of the grave. Outside were poverty and resentment, the recollection of the rigours of Pentonville Prison, a sense of injustice. Old Lyne slept on the first floor. His bed was between these two high windows. That lower window marked the study where he sat in the daytime. There was a safe in the wall, full of useless old papers. Old Lyne never kept money in the house. All his life he had advertised this habit. A burglar or two had gone to enormous trouble to prove him a liar and had got nothing for their pains.

There he was, sleeping in luxury, the old rat, under featherweight blankets specially woven for him, under a satin coverlet packed tight with rare down, and here was he, Horace Tom Tickler, with a pinch of silver in his pocket.

But, perhaps he was not there at all? That was an old trick of his, to be out when everybody thought he was in, and in when they thought he was out.

He walked up and down the quiet cul-de-sac for nearly an hour, turning over in his mind numerous schemes, mostly impracticable, then he slouched back towards the bright streets and coffee stalls. He took a short cut through the mews to reach Portland Place, and the most astounding luck was with him.

A policeman walking through Baynes Mews heard the sound of a man singing. It was, if his hearing gave a right impression, the voice of one who had gone far in insobriety, and the voice came from a tiny flat, one of the many above the garages that lined each side of the mews. Time was when they were occupied exclusively by coachmen and chauffeurs, but the artistic and aristocratic classes had swamped these humble West End habitations, and more than half of the new population of Baynes Mews were people who dressed for dinner and came home from parties and night clubs, their arms filled with gala favours, some of which made strange and distressing noises.

There was nothing in the voice to indicate anything more startling than normal inebriety. The policeman would have passed on but for the fact that he saw a figure sitting on the step of the narrow door which led to the little flat above.

The officer turned his electric lamp on the sitter and saw nothing which paid for illumination. The little man who grinned up at the policeman was, as the officer said to his sergeant later, "nothing to write home about." He was red-faced, unshaven, wretchedly shabby. His collar might have been white a week before; he wore no tie and his linen, even in the uncertain light of the lamp, was uncleanly.

" 'Ear him?" He jerked his head upward and grinned. "First time it's ever happened. Soused! What a mug, eh? Gettin' soused. He slipped me tonight, an' I'd never have tailed him – but for this bit of luck... 'Eard him by accident... Soused!"

"You're a bit soused yourself, aren't you?"

The policeman's tone was unfriendly.

"I've had three whiskies and a glass of beer. Does a man of the world get soused on that, I ask you?"

The voice upstairs had died down to a deep hum.

At the far end of the mews a horse was kicking in his box with maddening irregularity.

"A friend of yours?"

The little man shook his head.

"I don't know. Perhaps; that's what I got to find out. Is he friendly or ain't he?"

The policeman made a gesture.

"Get out of this. I can't have you loungin' about. I seem to know your face, too. Didn't I see you at Clerkenwell Police Court once?"

This officer prided himself on his memory for faces. It was his practice to say that he could never remember names, but never forgot faces. He thought he was unique and his remark original, and was not conscious of being one of forty million fellow citizens who also remembered faces and forgot names.

The little man rose and fell in by the officer's side.

"That's right." His step was a little unsteady. "I got nine munce for fraud."

He had in truth been convicted of petty larceny and had gone to prison for a month, but thieves have their pride.

Could a man convicted of fraud be arrested under the Prevention of Crimes Act because he sat in the doorway of a mews flat? This was the problem that exercised the mind of the constable. At the end of the mews he looked round for his sergeant, but that authority was not in sight.

A thought occurred to him.

"What you got in your pocket?"

The little man stretched out his arms.

"Search me – go on. You ain't entitled to, but I'll let you."

Another dilemma for the policeman, who was young and not quite sure of his rights and duties.

"Push off. Don't let me see you hanging around here," he ordered.

If the little man argued or refused he could be arrested for "obstruction," for "insulting behaviour," for almost anything. But he did nothing.

"All right," he said, and walked off.

The policeman was tempted to recall him and discover the identity of the singer. Instead, he watched Mr Tickler until he was out of sight.

The hour was a quarter to two in the morning. The patrol marched on to the point where his sergeant would meet him. As for Mr Tickler, he went shuffling down Portland Place, looking in every doorway to find a cigarette end or cigar butt, which might have been dropped by returning householders.

What a tale to tell if he could sell the information in the right quarter! Or he could put the "black" upon the singer. Blackmail gets easy money – if there is money to get. He stopped at a stall in Oxford Circus and drank a scalding cup of coffee. He was not entirely without funds and had a bed to go to and money for bus fare, if the buses were running.

Refreshed, he continued his way down Regent Street and met the one man in the world he would willingly have avoided. Surefoot Smith was standing in the shadow of a recessed shop window, a stocky man, in a tightly buttoned overcoat. His derby hat was, as usual, on the back of his head; his round face ruddier than Mr Tickler's was impassive. But for the periodical puffs of smoke which came from his big briar pipe he might have been a statue carved out of red brick.

"Hey!"

Reluctantly Tickler turned. He had been quick to identify the silent watcher. By straightening his shoulders and adding something of jauntiness to his stride he hoped to prevent the recognition from becoming mutual.

Surefoot Smith was one of the few people in the world who have minds like a well-organised card index. Not the smallest and least important offender who had passed through his hands could hope to reach a blissful oblivion.

"Come here – you."

Tickler came.

"What are you doing now, Tickler? Burglary, or just fetching the beer for the con men? Two a.m! Got a home?"

"Yes Sir."

"Ah, somewhere in the West End! Gone scientific, maybe. Science is the ruin of the country!"

Rights or no rights, he passed his hands swiftly over Tickler's person; the little man stretched out his arms obediently and smiled. It was not a pretty smile, for his teeth were few and his mouth large and lop-sided. But it was a smile of conscious virtue.

"No jemmy, no chisel, no bit, no gat." Surefoot Smith gave Mr Tickler absolution.

"No, Mr Smith; I'm runnin' straight now. I'm going after a job tomorrow."

"Don't waste my time, boy," said Surefoot reproachfully. "Work! You've read about it. What kind of thieving do you do now? Whizzing? No, you're not clever enough."

Tickler said a bold thing. The lees of wine were still sizzling within him. "I'm a detective," he said.

If Surefoot Smith was revolted he did not betray his emotion.

"Did you say 'defective' or 'detective'?" he asked.

He might have asked further questions, but at that moment a pocket lamp flashed twice from the roof of the building he was watching. Instantly the roadway seemed to be covered by the figures of overcoated men converging on the building. Surefoot Smith was one of the first to reach the opposite sidewalk.

A loud rapping on the door told Mr Tickler all he wanted to know. The place was being raided – a spieling club, or maybe worse. He was grateful for the relief and hurried on his way. At Piccadilly Circus he paused and considered matters. He was quite sober now and could review the position calmly; and the more he thought, the more thoroughly he realised that he had allowed opportunity to slip past him.

He turned and walked along Piccadilly, his chin on his chest, dreaming dreams of easy money.

3

Mary Lane looked at the plain gold watch on her wrist and gasped.

"Four o'clock, my dear!"

There were still twenty couples on the dancing floor of the Legation Club. It was a gala night, and they kept late hours at the Legation on these occasions.

"Sorry you've had such a tiring evening."

Dick Allenby didn't look sorry; he certainly did not look tired. There were no shadows under the laughing grey eyes, the tanned face was unlined. Yet he had not seen his bed for twenty-four hours.

"Anyway, you rescued me," he said as he called a waiter. "Think of it! I was alone until you came. When I said Moran had been and gone I was lying. The devil didn't turn up. Jerry Dornford tried to edge in on the party – he's still hoping."

He glanced across to a table on the other side of the room where the immaculately dressed Jerry sat.

"I hardly know him," she said.

Dick smiled.

"He wants to know you better – but he is distinctly a person not to know. Jerry has been out all the night – went away just before supper and has only just come back. Your other party was dull, was it? Funny devil, this man Wirth. It was cheek of Mike Hennessey to invite you there."

"Mike is rather a dear," she protested.

"Mike is a crook – a pleasant crook, but a crook. Whilst he is at large it is disgraceful that there is anybody else in prison!"

They passed out into the street, and as they stood waiting for a cab Dick Allenby saw a familiar figure.

"Why, Mr Smith, you're out late!"

"Early," said Surefoot Smith. He lifted his hat to the girl. "Evening, Miss Lane. Shockin' habit, night clubs."

"I'm full of bad habits," she smiled. Here was another man she liked. Chief Inspector Smith of Scotland Yard was liked by many people and heartily disliked by many more.

The cab drew up. She refused Dick's escort any further and drove off.

"Nice young lady that," said Surefoot. "Actresses don't mean anything to me – I've just come from Marlborough Street, where I've been chargin' three of 'em – at least, they called themselves actresses."

"A little raid?"

"A mere nothing," said Surefoot sadly. "I expected to find kings and only pulled in prawns."

"Pawns," suggested Dick.

"Small fish, anyway," said Surefoot.

That he was called "Surefoot" was no testimony to his gifts as a sleuth. It was his baptismal name. His father had been a bookmaking publican, and a month before his child was born the late Mr Smith, obsessed with the conviction that Surefoot, the Derby favourite, would not win, had laid that horse to win himself a fortune. If Surefoot had won, the late Mr Smith would have been a ruined man. Surefoot lost, and in gratitude he had named his infant child after the equine unfortunate.

"I nearly came up to your workshop the other day and had a squint at that gun of yours – air-gun, ain't it?"

"A sort of one," said Dick. "Who told you about it?"

"That feller Dornford. *He's* a bad egg! I can't understand it – your gun. Dornford says you put in a cartridge and fire it, and that charges the gun."

"It compresses the air – yes."

Dick Allenby was not in the mood to discuss inventions.

"You ought to sell it to Chicago," said Mr Smith, and made a clicking noise with his lips. "Chicago! Six murders a week and nobody pinched!"

Dick laughed. He had only returned from Chicago a month before and he knew something of the problems that the police had to face.

"These ride murders," Surefoot went on. "I mean takin' fellers out into the country in a car and shootin' 'em. Would it be possible here? No!"

"I'm not so sure." Dick shook his head. "Anyway, it is nearly half-past four and I'm not going to talk crime with you. Come up to my flat and we'll have a drink."

Surefoot Smith hesitated.

"All right; there's no sleep for me tonight. There's a cab."

The cab stood in the middle of the road near an island.

Smith whistled.

"Driver's gone away, sir." It was the club linkman who offered the information. "I tried to get it for the lady."

"He's asleep inside," said Smith, and walked across the road, Dick following.

Surefoot peered through the closed window of the cab, but saw nothing.

"He's not there," he said, and looked again. Then he turned the handle and pulled open the door. Somebody was there – somebody lying on the floor, with his legs on the seat.

"Drunk!" said Smith.

He flashed his lamp on the figure. The face was visible, yet indistinguishable, for he had been shot through the head at close quarters; but Smith saw enough to recognise something which had once been Mr Horace Tom Tickler and was now just a dead, mangled thing.

"Taken for a ride!" gasped Surefoot. "Good God! What's this – Chicago?"

4

In five minutes there were a dozen policemen round the cab, holding back the crowd which had gathered, as crowds will gather at any hour of the day or night in London. Fortunately, a police sergeant had been at Marlborough Street, attending to a drunk, and he was on the spot within a few minutes.

"Shot at close quarters by a very small-bore pistol," was his first verdict after a casual examination.

In a very short time the ambulance arrived, and all that was mortal of Horace Tom Tickler was removed. A police officer started up the engine of the taxi and drove it into the station yard for closer inspection. The number had already been taken. Scotland Yard had sent a swift car to find the owner, a taxi driver named Wells.

Dick Allenby had not been specifically invited to the investigations, but had found himself in conversation with Surefoot Smith at crucial moments of the search, and had drifted with him to the police station.

The man had been shot in the cab; they found a bullet hole through the leather lining of the hood. The body, Smith thought, had sagged forward to the ground and the legs had been lifted in the approved gang style.

"He was probably still alive when he was on the floor. The murderer must have fired a second shot. We have found a bullet in the floor-board of the cab."

"Have you found the driver?" asked Dick.

"He's on his way."

Mr Wells, the driver, proved to be a very stout and thoroughly alarmed man. His story was a simple one. He had got to the garage where he kept his car a little before two o'clock. The door of the garage was closed. He left the cab outside, which was evidently a practice of his, for the cleaner, who would come on duty at six o'clock and prepare the cab for the day's work. He could leave it outside with impunity, because cabs are very rarely stolen; they are so easily identified and so useless to the average car thief that they are very seldom "knocked off." His garage was in a stable yard off the Marylebone Road.

So far as he was concerned, he had a complete alibi, for, after leaving the cab, he had gone to the nearest police station to deposit an umbrella and a pocket-book which had been left by a previous passenger. A policeman had seen him leave the car, and to this policeman he had brought the lost property, which he had afterwards deposited at the station. It was a very lonely yard, and, unlike such places, was entirely without inhabitants, the garages forming part of a building which was used as a furniture store.

It was seven o'clock, and the West End was alive with market cars, when Dick drove home to his flat at Queen's Gate. It was curious that the only impression left on him was one of relief that Mary had not walked across the road to the cab and opened the door, as she might have done, and made the hideous discovery. The car had been parked outside the club twenty minutes before the discovery; the driver had been seen to leave the taxi and walk towards Air Street.

The earliest discovery that had been made was that the taxi flag was down and a sum of seventeen shillings was registered on the clock. This gave the police approximately the period between the murder being committed and the body being found.

Late that afternoon Surefoot Smith called on Dick Allenby.

"Thought you'd like to know how far we've got," he said. "We found a hundred one-pound notes in this bird's pocket."

"Tickler's?"

"How did you know his name was Tickler?" Surefoot Smith regarded him with suspicion.

Dick did not answer immediately.

"Well, the odd thing is, I recognised him when I saw him. He used to be a servant of my uncle's."

"You didn't tell me that last night."

"I wasn't sure last night; I wasn't sure, in fact, until I saw the body lifted out. I don't know very much about my uncle's business, but I understand this man was fired for stealing, about six or seven years ago."

Surefoot nodded.

"That's right. I'd come to give you that bit of information. I saw old Lyne this morning, but, bless you, Scotland Yard means nothing to him. Your uncle, is he?" He nodded again. "Congratulations!"

"What did he say?" asked Dick, curious.

Surefoot Smith lit his huge pipe.

"If you think he broke down, I am here to put you right. All he could remember about Tickler was that he was a scoundrel, and anyway we knew that. A hundred one-pound notes! If there had only been a fiver amongst them it might have been easy."

He cleared a space on a crowded bench and perched himself upon it.

"I wonder who the fellow was who took him for a ride? American, I'll bet you! That's what's worrying me – science coming into crime!"

Dick laughed.

"According to you, Surefoot, science is responsible for all crime."

Mr Smith raised his eyebrows enquiringly.

"Well, isn't it? What's science done? It's given us photography to make forgery easy, aeroplanes to get thieves out of the country, motor-cars for burglars. What's wireless done? I've had four cases in the West End in the last six months of fellows who used wireless to rob people! What's electricity done? It helps safe smashers to drill holes in strong rooms! Science!"

Dick thought there was very little evidence of applied science in the taxicab murder, and said so.

"It might have been committed in a horse cab."

"The driver couldn't have left a horse," was the crushing retort. "I'll bet you this is the first of many."

He reached out and put his hand on the oblong steel box that lay on the bench near him.

"That's science, and therefore it's going to be used by criminals. It's a noiseless gun – "

"Was the pistol last night noiseless?" asked Dick.

Surefoot Smith thought a moment, and then:

"Have you got any beer?" he asked.

There were a dozen bottles under one of the benches. Dick had many visitors who required refreshment. Surefoot Smith opened two and drank them in rapid succession. He was a great drinker of beer, had been known to polish off twenty bottles at a sitting without being any the worse for it, claiming, indeed, that beer intensified his powers of reasoning.

"No," he said, and wiped his moustache carefully with a large red handkerchief; "and yet we have seen nobody who heard the shots. Where were they fired? That cab could have been driven somewhere in the country. There are plenty of lonely places where a couple of shots would not be noticed or heard. You can go a long way in a couple of hours. There were rain marks on the windscreen and mud on the wheels. There was no rain in London; there has been a lot just outside of London."

He reached mechanically under the bench, took out a third and a fourth bottle and opened them absent-mindedly.

"And how did you find my noble relative?"

"Friend of yours?" asked Surefoot.

Dick shook his head.

"Well, I can tell you what I think of him."

Mr Smith described Hervey Lyne in a pungent sentence.

"Very likely," agreed Dick Allenby, watching his beer vanish. "I'm hardly on speaking terms with him."

Again Surefoot wiped his moustache with great care.

"This fellow Tickler – you had a few words with him, didn't you, about five years ago?"

Dick's eyes narrowed.

"Did Mr Lyne tell you that?"

"Somebody told me," said Surefoot vaguely.

"I kicked him out of my flat, yes. He brought rather an insulting message from my uncle, and supplemented it with a few remarks of his own."

Surefoot got down from the bench and brushed himself carefully.

"You ought to have told me all this last night," he said reproachfully. "It might have saved me a bit of trouble."

"I also might have saved myself four bottles of beer," said Dick, slightly irritated.

"That's been put to a good use," said Surefoot.

He examined the odd-looking airgun again, lifted it without difficulty and replaced it.

"That might have done it," he said.

"Are you suggesting I killed this fellow?" Dick Allenby's anger was rising.

Surefoot smiled.

"Don't lose your temper. It's not you I am up against, but science."

"It certainly is a gun," said Dick, controlling his wrath; "but the main idea – I don't know whether you can get it into your thick head – "

"Thank you," murmured Surefoot.

"– is that this should be put to commercial use. By exploding an ordinary cartridge, or nearly an ordinary cartridge, in this breech, I create a tremendous air pressure, which can be just as well used for running a machine as for shooting a gaol-bird."

"You knew he'd been in gaol?" asked Surefoot, almost apologetically.

"Of course I knew he'd been in gaol – two or three times, I should imagine, but I only know of one occasion, when my uncle prosecuted him. If I were you, Surefoot, I'd go to Chicago and learn something of the police methods there – "

19

"There ain't any," interrupted Surefoot decidedly. "I've studied the subject."

As Surefoot Smith walked towards Hyde Park he observed that all other events in the world had slumped to insignificance by the side of the taxicab murder. Every newspaper bill flamed with the words. One said "Important Clue"; he wasted a penny to discover that the clue was the first news that a hundred pounds had been found in the dead man's pocket, a fact which had not previously been revealed.

The antecedents of Wells had been investigated during the day and he had been given a clean bill by a man whose chief desire was to find the most damning evidence against him.

Smith was due at Scotland Yard for a conference at four o'clock. He hated conferences, where people sat round and smoked and expressed extravagant views on subjects they knew nothing about. But on this occasion, the first time for many years, he arrived promptly and had the satisfaction of finding that his four colleagues were as barren of ideas as he. They knew – and this was no discovery – that there was a possibility that this was a new type of crime which might become prevalent. Desperadoes had before now stolen cars, but had confined their operations to minor out-of-town burglaries.

There was one scrap of news. A policeman patrolling Portland Place from one of the mews behind had identified the body as that of a man to whom he had spoken at a quarter to two, and this tallied with Smith's own knowledge, for it was at two o'clock that he had seen Tickler walking down Regent Street from the direction of Portland Place.

Curiously enough, though a familiar phenomenon to police investigators, the policeman had said nothing about the drunken man in whose voice Tickler had been interested. Nor, in his report, had he given so much as a hint of that part of the conversation which revealed his knowledge of a man against whom he had had a grudge, and who might conceivably have had as deep an animosity towards him.

"This tells me no more than I know," said Surefoot, putting down the report. "Except that it is not true that Tickler ever had nine months; all his sentences were shorter. Who was it killed this poor little hound? He was broke, or nearly broke. I saw him stop to pick up a cigarette from the sidewalk just before he came up to me. Who picked him up in the stolen cab, and why?"

Fat McEwan leaned back in his well-filled chair and blew a trumpet of smoke to the ceiling.

"If there were such things as gangs you could guess it at once," he said despairingly. "But there are no gangs. This man was not even a nose, was he, Surefoot?"

Surefoot shook his head. "A nose" is a police informer, and Tickler had never been that.

"Then why the dickens should he have been killed? Tell me that."

This was a fair summary of an hour's discussion. Surefoot Smith went down to his little office entirely unenlightened. He found a number of letters, and one that had been posted at Westminster and had been delivered that afternoon. The envelope was dirty; his address was scrawled in an illiterate hand. He tore open the envelope and took out a sheet of paper, obviously extracted from a memorandum book of the cheaper kind. In pencil were the words:

"If you want to know who killed poor Mr Tickler you'd better go and have a talk with Mr L Moran."

Smith looked at the letter for a long time, and then: "Why not?" he asked himself aloud.

There were a great many things about Mr Moran that he could never quite understand.

21

5

Faith needs the garnishing of romance as much as hope requires the support of courage. Mary Lane had faith in her future, courage to brace the hope of ultimate achievement. Otherwise she was without the more important and disastrous illusions which do so much to create rosy prospects and unhappy memories.

She knew that some day she would be accepted by the West End of London as an important actress, that her name would appear in electric lights outside a theatre, and a little larger than her fellow artistes on the day-bill. But she never dreamed vain dreams of sudden fame, though, in the nature of things, fame is as sudden as the transition of a sound sleeper to wakefulness. Some day the slumbering public would open its eyes and be aware of Mary Lane. In the meantime it was oblivious of her existence – all except a few wide-awake writers of dramatic criticism. These very few, having a weakness for discovery, continuously swept the theatrical sky in search of nth dimension stars which would one day (here the astronomical analogy became absurd) blaze into the first dimension. Occasionally they "found"; more often than not they made themselves ridiculous, but covered their failure with well-designed fun poked at themselves and their own enthusiasms – which is one of the tricks of their business.

It was only a half-hearted discovery so far as Mary was concerned. She was a brighter speck in the nebula of young actresses. She might be (they said) a very great actress some day, if she overcame her habit of dropping her voice, if she learned how to use her hands, if this, that and the other.

Mary strove diligently, for she was at the age when dramatic critics seem infallible. She did not dream unprofitably; never lay awake at night, imagining the eruption of an agitated management into the dressing-room she shared with two other girls.

"You're understudying Miss Fortescue, aren't you? Get into her clothes quick: she's been taken ill."

She did not visualise newspaper columns acclaiming the young actress who had found fame in a night. She knew that understudy performances, however politely received, are as politely forgotten, and that a girl who grows famous in an evening steps into oblivion between Saturday and Monday.

On the second morning after her appearance at Washington Wirth's party, she had a brief interview with Mr Hervey Lyne on the subject of her allowance. It was not a pleasant interview. None of her interviews with Mr Lyne had ever been that.

"If you go on the stage you must expect to starve!" he snarled. "Your fool of a father made me his executor and gave me full authority. A hundred and fifty a year is all that you get until you're twenty-five. And there is nothing more to be said!"

She was very pretty and very angry, but she kept her temper admirably.

"Twenty thousand pounds brings in more than a hundred and fifty a year," she said.

He glared in her direction; she was just a blotch of blue and pink to his myopic vision.

"It is all you will get until you are twenty-five – and then I'll be glad to get rid of you. And another thing, young lady: you're a friend of my nephew, Richard Allenby?"

Her chin went up.

"Yes."

He wagged a skinny forefinger at her.

"He gets nothing from me – whether I'm alive or dead. Understand that!"

She did not trust herself to reply.

Binny showed her out and was incoherently sympathetic.

"Don't worry, miss," he said in his dull voice; "he ain't himself this mornin'."

She said nothing, hardly noticed Binny, who sighed heavily and wagged his head mournfully as he shut the door. He was by way of being a sentimentalist.

Ten minutes later she was talking vehemently over the telephone to Dick Allenby. His sympathy was more acceptable.

People used to say about Hervey Lyne that he was the sort of character that only Dickens could have drawn, which is discouraging to a lesser chronicler. He was eccentric in appearance and habit; naturally so, because he was old and self-willed and had a vivid memory of his past importance.

Everybody who was anybody in the late Victorian age had borrowed money from Hervey Lyne, and most of them had paid it back with considerable interest. Unlike the late "Chippy" Isaacs, as mild and pleasant a gentleman as ever issued money on note of hand, Hervey was harsh, unconscionable and rude. But he was quick. The swells who drove in broughams and had thousands on their horses, and gave champagne parties to men who wore side whiskers and women who wore flounces and regarded other women who smoked cigarettes as being damned body and soul, were sometimes in difficulties to find ready money, and generally they chose Hervey first because they knew their fate sooner than if they applied to Chippy.

Hervey said "No" or "Yes," and meant "No" or "Yes." You could go into Hervey's parlour in Naylors Crescent and either come out in five minutes with the money you needed or in two minutes with the sure knowledge that if you had stayed two hours you would not have persuaded him.

He gave up lending money when the trustees of the Duke of Crewdon's estate fought him in the Law Courts and lost. Hervey thought they would win, and had the shock of his life. Thereafter he only lent very occasionally, just as a gambler will play cards occasionally (and then for small stakes) to recover something of the old thrill.

His attitude to the world can be briefly defined: the galley of his life floated serenely on a sluggish sea of fools. His clients were fools; he had never felt the least respect for any of them. They were fools to borrow, fools to agree to enormous and staggering rates of interest, fools to repay him.

Dick Allenby was a fool, a pottering inventor and an insolent cub who hadn't the brains to see on which side his bread was buttered. Mary Lane was a fool, a posturing actress who painted her face and kicked her legs about (he invariably employed this inelegant illustration) for a pittance. One was his nephew, and might with tact have inherited a million; the other was the daughter of his sometime partner, and might, had she been a good actress, have enjoyed the same inheritance – would enjoy it yet if he could arouse himself from his surprising lethargy and alter his will.

His servants were complete fools. Old Binny, bald, stout, perspiring, who pulled his bath-chair into the park and read him to sleep, was a fool. He might have taken a kindlier view of Binny and left him a hundred or so "for his unfailing loyalty and tireless services," but Binny hummed hymn tunes in the house and hummed them a key or so flat.

Not that Binny cared. He was a cheery soul with large eyes and a completely bald head. A bit of a sluggard, whom his thin and whining wife (who was also the cook of 17, Naylors Crescent) found a difficult man to get out of bed in the mornings. Valet, confidential servant, messenger, butler, chair-puller, and reader, Binny, alert or sleepy, was worth exactly three times as much wages as he received.

Old Hervey sat propped up in his armchair, glooming at the egg and toast that had been put before him. His thin old face wore an expression of discontent. The thick, tinted glasses which hid the hard blue eyes were staring at the tray, and his mind was far away.

"Has that jackass of a detective called again?"

"No, sir," said Binny. "You mean Mr Smith?"

"I mean the fool that came to ask questions about that blackguard Tickler," stormed the old man emphasising every sentence with a blow on the table that set the cups rattling.

"The man who was found in the cab – ?"

"You know who I mean," snarled the old man. "I suppose one of his thieving friends killed him. It's the sort of end a man like that would come to."

Hervey Lyne relapsed into silence, a scowl on his face. He wondered if Binny was robbing him too. There had been a suspicious increase in the grocery bill lately, Binny's explanation that the cost of food had gone up being entirely unacceptable. And Binny was one of those smooth, smug, crawling slaves who wouldn't think twice about robbing an employer. It was about time Binny was changed. He had hinted as much that morning, and Binny had almost moaned his anguish.

"It's going to be a fine day, sir, for your outing." He stirred the contents of the teapot surreptitiously with a spoon.

"Don't talk," snapped the old man.

There was another long silence, and then: "What time is that fellow calling?" he asked harshly.

Binny, who was pouring out the tea at a side table, turned his big head and gazed pathetically at his employer.

"What feller, sir? The young lady came at nine – "

Hervey's thin lip curled in silent fury.

"Of course she did, you fool! But the bank manager…didn't you ask him to come – "

"At ten, sir – Mr Moran – "

"Get the letter – get it!"

Binny placed the cup of tea before his employer, rummaged through a small heap of papers on an open secretaire and found what he sought.

"Read it – read it!" snapped the old man. "I can't be bothered."

He never would be bothered again. He could tell light from dark; knew by a pale blur where the window was, could find his way unaided up the seventeen stairs which led to his bedroom, but no more. He could sign his name, and you would never suspect that a man more than half blind was responsible for that flourish.

"DEAR MR LYNE" (*read Binny in the monotonous voice he adopted for reading aloud*), – "I will give myself the pleasure of calling on you at ten o'clock tomorrow morning.

"Yours faithfully,
"LEO MORAN."

Hervey smiled again.

"Give himself the pleasure, eh?" His thin voice grew shrill. "Does he think I'm asking him here for his amusement? There's the door bell."

Binny shuffled out and came back in a few seconds with the visitor.

"Mr Moran," he announced.

"Sit down – sit down, Mr Moran." The old man waved a hand vaguely. "Find him a chair, Binny, and get out – d'ye hear? Get out! And don't listen at the door, damn you!"

The visitor smiled as the door closed on a Binny who was unconcerned, unemotional, unresentful.

"Now, Moran – you're my bank manager."

"Yes, Mr Lyne. I asked if I could see you a year ago, if you remember – "

"I remember," testily. "I don't want to see bank managers: I want them to look after my money. That is your job – you're paid for it, handsomely, I've no doubt. You have brought the account?"

The visitor took an envelope from his pocket, and, opening it, brought out two folded sheets of paper.

"Here – " he began, and his chair creaked as he rose.

"I don't want to see them – just tell me what is my balance."

"Two hundred and twelve thousand seven hundred and sixty pounds and a few shillings."

"M'm!" The "m'm" was a purr of satisfaction. "That includes the deposit, eh? And you hold stock…?"

"The stock held amounts to six hundred and thirty-two thousand pounds."

"I'll tell you why I want you – " began Lyne; and then, suspiciously: "Open the door and see if that fellow's listening."

The visitor rose, opened the door and closed it again.

"There's nobody there," he said.

He was slightly amused, though Mr Lyne's infirmities prevented him from observing this fact.

"Nobody, eh? Well, Moran, I'll tell you candidly: I regard myself as a remarkably able man. That is not boastful, it is a fact which you yourself could probably verify. I trust nobody – not even bank managers. My eyesight is not as good as it was, and it is a little difficult to check up accounts. But I have a remarkable memory. I have trained myself to carry figures in my head, and I could have told you to within a few shillings exactly the figures that you gave to me."

He paused, stared through his thick glasses in the direction of the man who sat at the other side of his desk.

"You're not a speculator or a gambler?"

"No, Mr Lyne, I am not."

A pause.

"H'm! That fool Binny was reading to me a few days ago the story of a bank manager who had absconded, taking with him a very considerable sum. I confess I was uneasy. People have robbed me before – "

"You are not being very polite, Mr Lyne."

"I'm not trying to be polite," snapped the old man. "I am merely telling you what has happened to me. There was a scoundrelly servant of mine, a fellow called Tickler. The fellow who was killed…"

He rambled on, a long, long story about the minor depredations of his dishonest servant, and the man who called himself Moran listened patiently. He was very relieved when he had taken the thin, limp hand in his and the door of No. 17, Naylors Crescent, closed behind him.

"Phew!" he said. He had a habit of speaking his thoughts aloud. "I wouldn't go through that again for a lot of money."

Binny, summoned from the deeps by a bell, came in to find the visitor gone.

"What does he look like, Binny? Has he an honest face?"

Binny thought profoundly.

"Just a face," he said vaguely, and the old man snorted.

"Clear those breakfast things away. Who else is coming to see me?"

Binny thought for a long time.

"A man named Dornford, sir."

"A gentleman named Dornford," corrected his master. "He owes me money, therefore he is a gentleman. At what hour?"

"About eight o'clock, sir."

Lyne dismissed him with a gesture.

At three o'clock that afternoon he ambled out of his sitting-room, wrapped in his thick Inverness coat and wearing his soft felt hat, allowed himself, growling complaints the while, to be tucked into his bath-chair, and was drawn painfully into the street; more painfully up the gentle slope to the park and into the private gardens, entry to which was exclusively reserved for tenants of Naylors and other terraces. Here he sat, under the shade of a tree, while Binny, perched uncomfortably upon a folding stool, read in his monotonous voice the happenings of the day.

Only once the old man interrupted.

"What time is Mr Dornford calling?"

"At eight o'clock, sir," said Binny.

Lyne nodded, pushed his blue-tinted glasses higher up the thin bridge of his nose and folded his gloved hands over the rug which protected his knees from errant breezes.

"You be in when he comes, d'ye hear? A tricky fellow – a dangerous fellow. You hear me, Binny?"

"Yes, sir."

"Then why the devil didn't you say so? Go on reading that trash."

Binny obeyed, and continued with great relish the story of London's latest murder. Binny was a great student of crime in the abstract.

6

Arthur Jules barely deserves description because he plays so small a part; but as that small part was big enough to put one man in the shadow of the gallows, he may be catalogued as a plump, sallow-faced young man, who wore a monocle, had perfectly brushed hair, and was invariably dressed as though he were on his way to a wedding reception.

He was a sort of attaché to a South American Legation, and a freelance of diplomacy generally. In more suspicious countries he would have been handed his passport with extreme politeness, and his departure from Southampton would have been watched by the bored detective whose business it is to superintend the shipment of oddities.

He was always important and profound; never more so than when he sat at the bay window overlooking St James's Street, stroking his little black moustache thoughtfully and speaking with just the slightest trace of an accent to Jerry Dornford.

Everybody knew and liked Jerry, whose other name was Gerald. He had all the qualities which endear a wastrel to the monied classes. He was, of course, a member of Snell's, as was Jules. He was, indeed, a member of all the important clubs where gentlemen meet. He paid his subscription, never passed a cheque which was dishonoured, had never been warned off or posted as a bankrupt. A tall man, with a slight stoop, brownish hair very thin on the top, deep-set eyes that smiled in a worn, tired face.

Jerry had lived very fast. Few of his creditors could keep up with him. He had been a co-respondent, and again a co-respondent, and was single, and lived in a little flat in Half Moon Street, where he gave small parties; very small. He retained his membership of exclusive racing clubs – bookmakers lived in the hope that he would one day settle with them. He had certain very rich relations who would certainly die, but were not so certain whether they would bequeath their undoubted wealth to this profligate son of Sir George Dornford. On the other hand, why shouldn't they?

He was in desperate need of money now. Jules knew how desperate: they had few secrets from one another. Whenever the little party in Half Moon Street was as many as four, Jules was the third.

"What is this fellow's name?"

"Hervey Lyne."

"Hervey Lyne? Yes, I know him. A very odd man," reminiscently. "When my dear father was Secretary of Legation – that must have been in 'ninety-three – he borrowed money from Lyne. But I thought he had retired from business. He was a moneylender, wasn't he?"

Jerry's lips twisted in an unpleasant smile.

"Financier," he said laconically. "Yes, he has retired. I owed him three thousand for years; it's four now. There was, of course, a chance that the dowager would leave a packet, but the old devil left it away, to the other side of the family."

"And he is pressing you?"

Jerry's jaw set.

"Yes," he said shortly. "To be exact, he is getting a judgment in bankruptcy, and I can't stop him. I have been dodging Carey Street all my life. Things have looked very black at times, but there has always been something that turned up."

There was a long and gloomy silence. Jules – he had another name, but nobody could remember it – stroked his little black moustache more quickly.

"Two thousand – that would stop the action, eh? Well, why not? Take two thousand, *et voilà!* There is nothing to it. I do not ask you, like the fellow in the story-books, to go to the War Office and rob them of their schemes of mobilisation. But I *do* want something, for a gentleman who has himself been working on the lines of your friend.

31

To me it seems a very large sum to pay for so small a thing. Naturally I do not say that to my gentleman. If he desires to be extravagant and my friend would benefit – *tiens*, why not?"

Jerry Dornford made a wry face at the street below. When he was asked to work for money he never forgot that he was a gentleman – it was rather a disgusting thing he was now asked to do, but he had contemplated things even more distressful. He had, in fact, found every solution to his difficulty except suicide.

"I am not so sure that it can be done, anyway," he said.

Two men came into the smoke-room. He looked up quickly and recognised both, but was interested particularly in one.

"That's Fate," he said.

"Who are they?" asked Jules.

He knew the second of the two, who was a member, but the first man, middle-aged, rather rotund, fair-haired, was a stranger to him.

"That's my bank manager. Incidentally, he is Lyne's banker too, a fellow named Moran – Major Moran, he loves to call himself. A Territorial fellow."

Jules shot a swift glance in the direction of the men who at that moment were seating themselves at the table.

"A great rifle shot. I saw him at Bisley. I was there with one of our generals, watching the shooting."

He turned his black eyes to Jerry.

"Well, my friend?"

Jerry breathed heavily through his nose and shook his head.

"I'll have to think it over," he said. "It's a beastly thing to do."

"More beastly to be a bankrupt, my friend," said Jules in his caressing voice. "Resignation from all clubs... Poor old Jerry, eh? You are going into the Mike Hennessey class. You don't want to be that."

"Why Mike Hennessey?" asked Jerry quickly, and the other laughed.

"An association of ideas. You go often to the Sheridan, eh? I do not blame you...a very charming girl."

He made a little grimace as though he were about to whistle.

"Association of ideas, eh? Allenby also likes the young lady. Queer how all things fit in, like the pieces of a puzzle. Think it over, my dear Jerry, and ring me up at the Grosvenor."

He snapped his fingers towards a club waiter, scribbled his initials on a bill and strolled towards the door, Jerry following. They had to pass Moran and his friend; that bluff, jolly-looking man looked up, nodded with careless friendliness and caught Jerry's sleeve as he was passing.

"I'd like to see you one day this week, if you're not busy, Jerry."

Jerry never forgot he was a member of Snell's and a gentleman. He never forgot that Mr Leo Moran was a sort of glorified bank clerk, who had probably had his education at the State's expense; and, knowing all these things, he resented the "Jerry." It added to his irritation that he knew why Mr Moran wished to see him. It was outrageous that one couldn't lunch in one's club without being dunned by cads of this description.

He pulled his sleeve away from the detaining finger and thumb.

"All right," he said.

He would have been more offensive if this man had not been a guest at the club, and, more important, if it were not in Moran's power to make things deucedly uncomfortable for Mr Gerald Dornford.

As he and Jules were passing down the stairs together…

"The swine! Who brought that kind of bird into the club? Snell's is getting impossible!"

Jules, who had a weakness for the rococo qualities of Italian opera, was humming a favourite aria of Puccini's. He smiled and shook his head.

"It takes all sorts of people to make a world, my friend," he said sententiously.

He flicked a speck from his immaculate coat sleeve, patted Jerry on the arm as though he were a child, and went swinging up St James's Street towards his mysterious Legation.

Jerry Dornford stood for a moment, hesitant, then walked slowly down towards the palace. He was in a jam, a tight jam, and it wasn't going to be so very easy to get out.

He obeyed an impulse, called a cab and drove to near Queen's Gate, where he alighted, paid his fare, and walked on.

Dick Allenby lived in a big house that had been converted into flats. There was no attendant on duty at the door, and the elevator that took him up to the fourth floor was automatic. He knocked at the door of Dick's studio – for studio it had once been, before Dick Allenby had converted it into a workroom. There was no answer, and he turned the handle and walked in. The room was empty. Evidently there had been visitors, for half a dozen empty beer bottles stood on a bench, though there was only one used tumbler visible. If he had known something of Surefoot Smith he might have reduced the visiting list to one.

"Are you there, Allenby?" he called.

There was no answer. He walked across to the bench where the odd-looking steel box lay, and lifted it. To his relief he found he could carry it without an effort. Putting it down again, he walked to the door. The key was on the inside; he drew it out and examined it carefully. If he had been an expert at the job he would have carried wax and taken an impression. As it was, his early technical training came to his aid – it had once been intended that he should follow the profession of engineer.

He listened; there was no sound of the lift moving. Dick, he knew, had his sleeping room on the upper floor, and was probably there now. Dornford made a rapid sketch on the back of an envelope – rapid but accurate. He judged the width of the key, made a brief note and replaced it as the sound of somebody coming down the stairs reached him.

He was standing examining the empty beer bottles when Dick came in.

"Hullo, Dornford!" There was no great welcome in the tone. "Did you want to see me?"

Jerry smiled.

"I was bored. I thought I'd come up and see what an inventor looked like. By the way, I saw you at the theatre the other night – nice girl that. She was damned rude to me the only time I spoke to her."

Dick faced him squarely.

"And I shall be damned rude to you the next time you speak to her," he said.

Jerry Dornford chuckled.

"Like that, eh? By the way, I'm seeing the old man tonight. Shall I give him your love?"

"He'd prefer that you gave him something more substantial," said Dick coldly.

It was a shot at a venture but it got home. Gerald the imperturbable winced.

It was odd that up to that moment Dick Allenby had never realised how intensely he disliked this man. There was excellent reason why he should hate him, but that was yet to be revealed.

"Why this sudden antagonism? After all, I've no feeling about this girl of yours. She's a jolly little thing; a bad actress, but a good woman. They don't go very far on the London stage – "

"If you're talking about Miss Lane I will bring the conversation to a very abrupt termination," said Dick; and then, bluntly: "Why did you come up here? You are quite right about the antagonism, but it is not very sudden, is it? I don't seem to remember that you and I were ever very great friends."

"We were in the same regiment, old boy – brother officers and all that," said Jerry flippantly. "Good Lord! It doesn't seem like twelve years ago – "

Dick opened the door and stood by it.

"I don't want you here. I don't particularly want to know you. If you see my uncle tonight you'd better tell him that: it will be a point in my favour."

Jerry Dornford smiled. His skin was thick, though he was very sensitive on certain unimportant matters.

"I suppose you knew this fellow Tickler who was killed the other night?" he began.

"I don't want even to discuss murders with you," said Dick.

He went out of the room, pulled open the door of the lift and shot back the folding iron gate. He was angry with himself afterwards that he had lost his temper, but he never knew the time when Jerry Dornford did not arouse a fury in him. He hated Jerry's views of life, his philosophy, the looseness of his code. He remembered Jerry's extraordinary dexterity with cards and a ruined subaltern who went gladly to his death rather than face the consequence of a night's play.

As he heard the elevator stop at the bottom floor he opened the window of the workshop to air it – an extravagant gesture, but one which accurately marked his attitude of mind towards his visitor.

7

The bank was closed, and Mr Moran had gone home, when Surefoot Smith called to make his enquiry.

Surefoot knew almost everybody who had any importance in London. Indeed, quite a number of people would have had a shock if they had known how very completely informed he was about their private lives. It is true that almost every man and woman in any civilised community has, to himself or herself, a criminal history. They may have broken no laws, yet there is guilt on their conscience; and it is a knowledge of this psychology which is of such invaluable aid to investigating detectives.

The nearest way to Parkview Terrace led him across the open end of Naylors Crescent. Glancing down, he saw a man coming towards him and stopped. Binny he knew to be an inveterate gossip, a great collector of stories and scandals, most of which were ill-founded. At the back of his mind, however, he associated Mr Lyne's serving man with the banker. Years before, Surefoot Smith had been in control of this division, and his memory was extraordinarily good.

"Good afternoon, Mr Smith."

Binny tipped his wide-brimmed bowler hat, and then, after a moment's hesitation: "May I be so bold to ask, sir, if there is any news?"

"You told me you knew this man Tickler?"

Binny shook his head.

"An acquaintance. He was my predecessor – "

"I'd have that word framed," said Surefoot Smith testily. "You mean he was the fellow who had your job before, don't you?" And, when

Binny nodded: "Then why didn't you say so? Didn't you work for Moran?"

Binny smiled.

"I've worked for almost every kind of gentleman," he said. "I was Lord Frenley's valet – "

"I don't want your family history, Binny," said Surefoot Smith. "What sort of man is Moran? Nice fellow – generous, eh? Free spender?"

Binny considered the matter as though his life depended upon his answer.

"He was a very nice gentleman. I was only with him for six months," he said. "He lives just round the corner, overlooking the park. In fact, you can see his flat from the gardens."

"A quiet sort of man?" asked Surefoot.

"I never heard him make much noise – " began Binny.

"When I say 'quiet,' " explained Surefoot Smith with a pained expression, "I mean, does he gad about? Women, wine, and song – you know the kind of thing I mean. I suppose your mother told you something when you were young?"

"I don't remember my mother," said Binny. "No, sir, I can't say that Mr Moran was a gadder. He used to have little parties – ladies and gentlemen from the theatre – but he gave that up after he lost his money."

Surefoot's eyes narrowed.

"Lost his money? He's a bank manager, isn't he? Had he any money to lose?"

"It was his own money, sir." Binny was shocked and hastened to correct a wrong impression. "That was why I left him. He had some shares in a bank – not his own bank but another one – and it went bust. I mean to say – "

"Don't try to interpret 'bust' to me. I know the word," said Surefoot. "Gave little theatrical parties like that fellow What's-his-name? Drinking and all that sort of thing?"

Binny could not help him. He was looking left and right anxiously, as though seeking a means of escape.

"In a hurry?" asked the detective.

"The big picture comes on in ten minutes; I don't want to miss it. It's Mary Pickford in – "

"Oh, her!" said Surefoot, and dismissed the world's sweetheart with a wave of his hand. "Now what about this man Tickler? Did he ever work for Moran?"

Binny considered this and shook his head.

"No, sir, I think he was working for Mr Lyne when I was with Mr Moran, but I'm not certain." And then, as a thought struck him: "He's on the wireless tonight."

Surefoot was staggered.

"Who?"

"Mr Moran. He's talking on economics or something. He often talks on banking and things like that – he's a regular lecturer."

Surefoot Smith was not very much interested in lecturers. He asked a few more questions about the unfortunate Tickler and went on his way.

Parkview Terrace was a noble block of buildings which had suffered the indignity in post-war days, as so many other buildings have suffered, of being converted into apartments. Mr Moran lived on the top flat, and he was at home, his servant told Surefoot when he came to the door. In point of fact he was dressing for dinner. Smith was shown into a large and handsome sitting-room, furnished expensively and with some taste. There were two windows which commanded a view of Regent's Park and the Canal, but it was the luxury of the appointments which arrested Surefoot's interest.

He knew the financial position of the average branch manager; could tell to within a few pounds just what their salaries were; and it was rather a shock to find even a twelve hundred a year manager living in an apartment which must have absorbed at least four hundred, and displaying evidence of wealth which men in his position have rarely the opportunity of acquiring.

A Persian carpet covered the floor; the electric fittings had the appearance of silver, and were certainly of the more exquisite kind that are not to be duplicated in a department store. There was a big

Knolle couch ("Cost a hundred," Smith noted mentally); in an illuminated glass case were a number of beautiful miniatures, and in another, rare ornaments of jade, some of which must have been worth a considerable sum.

Surefoot knew nothing about pictures, but he was satisfied that more than one of those on the wall were genuine Old Masters.

He was examining the cabinet when he heard a step behind him and turned to meet the owner of the flat. Mr Leo Moran was half-dressed and wore a silk dressing-gown over his shirt and white waistcoat.

"Hullo, Smith! We don't often see you. Sit down and have a drink." He rang the bell. "Beer, isn't it?"

"Beer it is," said Surefoot heartily. "Nice place you've got here, Mr Moran."

"Not bad," said the other carelessly. He pointed to a picture. "That's a genuine Corot. My father paid three hundred pounds for it, and it's probably worth three thousand today."

"Your father was well off, was he, Mr Moran?"

Moran looked at him quickly.

"He had money. Why do you ask? You don't imagine I could have furnished a flat like this on a thousand a year, do you?" His eyes twinkled. "Or has it occurred to you that this is part of my illicit gains – moneys pinched from the bank?"

"I hope," said Surefoot Smith solemnly, "that such a thought never entered into my head."

"Beer," said Mr Leo Moran, addressing the servant who had appeared in the doorway. "You've come about something, haven't you? What is it?"

Surefoot pursed his lips thoughtfully.

"I'm making enquiries about this man Tickler – "

"The fellow who was murdered. Do I know him, you mean? Of course I know him! The fellow was a pest. I never went from this house without finding him on the kerb outside, wanting to tell me something or sell me something – I have never discovered which."

He had a rapid method of speaking. His voice was not what Smith would have described as a gentleman's. Indeed, Leo Moran was very much of the people. His life had been an adventurous one. He had sailed before the mast, he had worked at a brass founder's in the Midlands, been in a dozen kinds of employment before he eventually drifted into banking. A rough diamond, with now and again a rough voice; more often, however, a suave one, for he had the poise and presence which authority and wealth bring. Now and again his voice grew harsh, almost common, and in moments he became very much a man of the people. It was in that tone he asked: "Do you suppose I killed him?"

Surefoot smiled; whether at the absurdity of the question or the appearance of a large bottle of beer and a tumbler, which were carried in at that moment, Moran was undecided.

"You know Miss Lane, don't you?"

"Slightly." Moran's tone was cold.

"Nice girl – here's luck." Surefoot raised his glass and swallowed its contents at a gulp. "Good beer, almost pre-war. Lord! I remember the time when you could get the best ale in the world for fourpence a quart."

He sighed heavily, and tried to squeeze a little more out of the bottle, but failed.

Moran touched the bell again. "Why do you ask me about Miss Lane?"

"I knew you were interested in theatricals – there's your servant."

"Another bottle of beer for Mr Smith," said Moran without turning his head. "What do you mean by theatricals?"

"You used to give parties, didn't you, once upon a time?"

The banker nodded.

"Years ago, in my salad days. Why?"

"I was just wondering," said Smith vaguely.

His host strode up and down the floor, his hands thrust into the silken pockets of his gown.

"What the devil did you come here for, Smith? You're not the sort of man to go barging round making stupid enquiries. Are you connecting me with this absurd murder – the murder of a cheap little gutter rat I scarcely know by sight?"

Surefoot shook his head.

"Is it likely?" he murmured.

Then the beer came, and Moran's fit of annoyance seemed to pass.

"Well, the least you can do is to tell me the strength of it – or aren't you enquiring about the murder at all? Come along, my dear fellow, don't be mysterious!"

Mr Smith wiped his moustache, got up slowly from the chair and adjusted his horrible pink tie before an old Venetian mirror.

"I'll tell you the strength of it, man to man," he said. "We had an anonymous letter. That was easy to trace. It was sent by Tickler's landlady, and it appeared that when he was very drunk, which was every day, sometimes twice a day, he used to talk to this good lady about you."

"About me?" said the other quickly. "But he didn't know me!"

"Lots of people talk about people they don't know," began Smith. "It's publicity – "

"Nonsense! I'm not a public man. I'm just a poor little bank manager, who hates banking, and would gladly pay a fortune, if he had one to pay, for the privilege of taking all the books of the bank and burning 'em in Regent's Park, making the clerks drunk, throwing open the vault to the petty thieves of London, and turning the whole damn thing into a night club!"

Gazing at him with open mouth, genuinely staggered by such a confession, Smith saw an expression in that sometime genial face that he had never seen before: a certain harshness; heard in his voice the vibration of a hidden fury.

"They nearly kicked me out once because I speculated," Moran went on. "I'm a gambler; I always have been a gambler. If they'd kicked me out I'd have been ruined at that time. I had to crawl on my hands and knees to the directors to let me stay on. I was managing a branch at Chalk Farm at the time, and I've had to pretend that the Northern and Southern Bank is something holy, that its directors are gods; and every time I've tried to get a bit of money so that I could clear out, the market has gone –!" He snapped his fingers. "I don't really know Tickler. Why he should talk about me I haven't the slightest idea."

Surefoot Smith looked into his hat.

"Do you know Mr Hervey Lyne?" he asked.

"Yes, he's a client of ours."

"Have you seen him lately?"

A pause, and then: "No, I haven't seen him for two years."

"Oh!" said Surefoot Smith.

He said "Oh!" because he could think of nothing else to say.

"Well, I'll be getting along. Sorry to bother you, but you know what we are at the Yard."

He offered his huge hand to the banker, but Mr Moran was so absorbed in his thoughts that he did not see it.

After Moran had closed the door upon his visitor he walked slowly back to his room and sat down on the edge of his bed. He sat there for a long time before he got up, walked across the room to a wall safe hidden behind a picture, opened it and took out a number of documents, which he examined very carefully. He put these back, and, groping, found a flat leather case which was packed with strangely coloured documents. They were train and steamship tickets; his passport lay handy, and, fastened in his passport by a thick rubber band, twenty banknotes for a hundred pounds.

He locked the safe again, replaced the picture, and went on with his dressing. He was more than a little perturbed. That casual reference to Hervey Lyne had shaken him.

8

At ten o'clock that night quite a number of wireless sets would be shut off at the item "The Economy of our Banking System," and would be turned on again at ten fifteen, when the Jubilee Jazz Band would be relayed from Manchester.

Binny read the programme through and came at last to the ten o'clock item.

"Moran. Is that the fellow who saw me yesterday?" asked the old man.

"Yes, sir," said Binny.

"Banking systems – bah!" snarled old Lyne. "I don't want to hear it. Do you understand, Binny? – I don't want to hear it!"

"No, sir," said Binny.

The white, gnarled hands groped along the table till they reached a repeater watch, and pressed a knob.

"Six o'clock. Get me my salad."

"I saw that detective today, sir – Mr Smith."

"Get me my salad!"

Chicken salad was his invariable meal at the close of day. Binny served him, but could do nothing right. If he spoke he was told to be quiet; if he relapsed into silence old Hervey cursed him for his sulkiness.

He had cleared away the meal, put a cup of weak tea before his master, and was leaving him to doze, when Lyne called him back.

"What are Cassari Oils?" he demanded. It was so long since Binny had read the fluctuations of the oil market that he had no information to give.

"Get a newspaper, you fool!"

Binny went in search of an evening newspaper.

It was his habit to read, morning and night, the movements of industrial shares; a monotonous proceeding, for Mr Lyne's money was invested in gilt-edged securities which were stately and steadfast and seldom moved except by thirty-seconds. Cassari Oils had been one of his errors. The shares had been part of a trust fund – he had hesitated for a long time before he converted them to a more stable stock. The period of his holding had been two years of torture to him, for they flamed up and down like a paper fire, and never stayed in one place for more than a week at a time.

Binny came back with the newspaper and read the quotation, which was received with a grunt.

"If they'd gone up I'd have sued the bank. That brute Moran advised me to sell."

"Have they gone up, sir?" asked Binny, interested.

"Mind your own business!" snapped the other.

Hervey Lyne used often to sit and wonder and fret himself over those Cassaris. They were founder's shares, not lightly come by, not easy to dispose of. The thought that he might have thrown away a fortune on the advice of a conservative bank manager, and that when he came to hand over his stewardship to Mary Lane he might be liable – which he would not have been – was a nightmare to him. The unease had been renewed that day by something which Binny had r   e   a   d to him from the morning newspaper concerning oil discoveries in Asia Minor.

In the course of the years he had accumulated quite a lot of data concerning the Cassari Oilfield, most of it very depressing to anybody who had money in the concern. He directed Binny to unearth the pamphlets and reports, and promised himself a possibly exasperating evening.

Eight o'clock brought a visitor, a reluctant man, who had rehearsed quite a number of plausible excuses. He had the feeling that he, being the last of the old man's debtors, was in the position of a mouse in the paws of an ancient cat, not to be killed too quickly; and here, to some extent, he was right.

Hervey Lyne received him with a set grin which was a parody of the smile he had used for so many years on such occasions.

"Sit down, Mr Dornford," he piped. "Binny, go out!"

"Binny's not here, Mr Lyne."

"He's listening outside the door – he's always listening. Have a look."

Dornford opened the door; there was no sign of the libelled servant.

"Now, now." Again he was his old business-like self, repeating a speech which was part of a formula. "About this money – three thousand seven hundred, I think. You're going to settle tonight?"

"Unfortunately I can't settle tonight, and not for many nights," said Jerry. "In fact, there's no immediate prospect of my settling at all. I've made arrangements to get you four or five hundred on account – "

"From Isaac and Solomon, eh?"

Jerry cursed himself for his stupidity. He knew that the moneylenders exchanged daily a list of proposals which had come to them.

"Well, you're not going to get it, my friend. You've got to find money to settle this account, or it goes into the hands of my collectors tomorrow."

Jerry had expected nothing better than this.

"Suppose I find you two thousand by the end of the week?" he said. "Will you give me a reasonable time to find the remainder?"

To his surprise he was speaking huskily – the imperturbable Jerry, who had faced so many crises with equanimity, was amazingly agitated in this, the most crucial of all.

"If you can find two thousand you can find three thousand seven hundred," boomed the old man. "A week? I wouldn't give you a day – and where are you getting the two thousand from?"

Jerry cleared his throat.

"A friend of mine – "

"That's a lie to begin with, Mr Gerald Dornford," said the hateful voice. "You have no friends; you've used them all up. I'll tell you what

I'll do with you." He leaned over the table, his elbows on the polished mahogany. He was enjoying this moment of his triumph, recovering some of the old values of a life that was now only a memory. "I'll give you till tomorrow night at six o'clock. Your money's here" – he tapped the table vigorously – "or I'll bankrupt you!"

If his sight had been only near to normal he would have seen the look that came into Jerry's face, and would have been frightened to silence. But, if he saw nothing, he sensed the effect of his words.

"You understand, don't you?"

Some of the steel went out of his tone.

"I understand." Jerry's voice was low.

"Tomorrow you bring the money, and I will give you your bill. A minute after six o'clock, and it goes to the collector."

"But surely, Mr Lyne" – Jerry found coherent speech at last – "two thousand pounds on account is not to be sniffed at."

"We shall see," said the old man, nodding. "I've nothing else to say."

Jerry rose; he was shaking with anger.

"I've got something to say, you damned old usurer!" He quivered with rage. "You bloodsucking old brute! You'll bankrupt me, will you?"

Hervey Lyne had come to his feet, his skinny hand pointing to the door.

"Get out!" His voice was little more than a whisper. "Bloodsucker …damned old usurer, am I? Binny – BINNY!"

Binny came stumbling up from the kitchen.

"Throw him out – throw him on his head – smash him!" screamed the old man.

Binny looked at the man who was head and shoulders taller than he, and his smile was sickly.

"Better get out, sir," he said under his breath, "and don't take no notice of me."

Then, in a louder, truculent tone: "Get out of here, will you?" He pulled open the street door noisily. "Out you get!"

He struck his palm with his fist, and all the time his imploring eyes begged the visitor to pardon his lapse of manners.

When he came back the moneylender was lying back, exhausted, in his chair.

"Did you hit him?" he asked weakly.

"Did I hit him, sir? I nearly broke me wrist."

"Did you break *his* wrist or anything else of him?" snarled Hervey, not at all interested in the injuries which might have come to the assailant.

"It'll take two doctors to put him right," said Binny.

The old man's thin lips curled in a sneer.

"I don't believe you touched him, you poor worm!" he said.

"Didn't you hear me – " began Binny, aggrieved.

"Clapping your hands together! Liar and fool, do you think I didn't know that? I may be blind but I've got ears. Did you hit the burglar last night – or when was it? You didn't even hear him."

Binny blinked at him helplessly. Two nights before somebody had smashed a glass at the back of the house and opened a window. Whether they succeeded in entering the kitchen or not it was impossible to say. Old Hervey, a light sleeper, heard the crash and came to the head of the stairs, screaming for Binny, who occupied a subterranean room adjoining the kitchen.

"Did you hit him? Did you hear him?"

"My idea was to bring in the police," began Binny. "There's nothing like the lor in cases like this…"

"Get out!" roared the old man. "The law! Do you think I wanted a lot of clumsy-footed louts in my house…get away, you make me sick!"

Binny left hurriedly.

For the greater part of two hours the old man sat, muttering to himself, twisting and untwisting his fingers one in the other; and then, as his repeater struck ten, he turned to the wireless set at his side and switched it on. A voice immediately blared at him…

"Before I discuss the banking systems of this country I would like to say a few words about the history of banking from the earliest times…"

Hervey Lyne sat up and listened. His hearing, as he had said, was extraordinarily sensitive.

9

Dick Allenby never described himself as being engaged, and the tell-tale finger of Mary Lane bore no ring indicative of her future. He mentioned the fact casually as he sat in her dressing-room between the last two acts of *Cliffs of Fate* and he talked to her through a cretonne curtain behind which she was changing her dress.

"I shall be getting a bad name," he said. "Nothing damages the reputation of an inventor more readily than to be recognised by stage-door keepers. He admits me now without question."

"Then you shouldn't come so often," she said, coming through the curtain, and sitting before her dressing-table.

"I won't say you're a matter of life and death to me," said Dick, "but very nearly. You're more important than anything in the world."

"Including the Allenby gun?"

"Oh, that!" he said contemptuously. "By the way, a German engineer came in today and offered me, on behalf of Eckstein's – they're the big Essen engineers – ten thousand pounds for the patent."

"What was the matter with him?" she asked flippantly.

"That's what I wondered," said Dick, lighting a forbidden cigarette. "No, he wasn't drunk – quite a capable bloke, and terribly discerning. He told me he thought I was one of the greatest inventors of the age."

"Darling, you are," she said.

"I know I am," said Dick complacently. "But it sounded awfully nice in German. Honestly, Mary, I had no idea this thing was worth so much."

"Are you selling it?" She turned her head to ask the question.

Dick hesitated.

"I'm not sure," he said. "But it is this enormous accession of wealth that has brought me to the point of your unadorned engagement finger."

She turned to the mirror, smoothed her face gently with a puff, and shook her head.

"I'm going to be a very successful actress," she said.

"You are a very successful actress," said Dick lazily. "You've extracted a proposal of marriage from a great genius."

She swung round in her chair.

"Do you know what I'm in dread of?" she asked.

"Besides marriage, nothing, I should think."

"No, there's one prospect that terrifies me." She was very serious. "And that is that your uncle should leave me all his money."

He chuckled softly.

"It is a fear that has never disturbed my night's rest – why do you say that?"

She looked at him, biting her lip thoughtfully.

"Once he said something about it, and it struck me quite recently that he loathes you so much that out of sheer pique he might leave it to me, and that would be dreadful."

He stared at her.

"In Heaven's name, why?" he asked.

"I should have to marry you," she said.

"Out of sheer pique?" he bantered.

She shook her head.

"No; but it would be dreadful, wouldn't it, Dick?"

"I think you're worrying yourself unnecessarily," he said dryly. "The old boy is more likely to leave it to a dog's home. Do you see much of him?"

She told him of her visit to Naylors Crescent, but that was old news to him.

They were talking when there came a tap at the door. She half rose, thinking it was the call boy; but when the knock was repeated and she said "Come in," it was Leo Moran who made an appearance.

He favoured Dick with a little grimace.

"Instead of wasting your time here you ought to be sitting at home, tuning in to my epoch-making address."

"Been broadcasting, have you?" smiled Dick. "Do they make you dress up for it?"

"I'm going on to supper."

This time the knock was followed by the singsong voice of the call boy, and Mary hurried out. She was glad to escape: for some reason she never felt quite at ease in Mr Moran's presence.

"Have you seen this show?" asked Dick.

Moran nodded.

"For my sins, yes," he said. "It's the most ghastly play in London. I wonder why old Mike keeps it on? He must have a very rich backer."

"Have you ever heard of Washington Wirth?"

Leo Moran's face was a blank.

"Never heard of him, no. What is he – an American?"

"Something unusual," said Dick. "I was reckoning up the other day; he must have lost ten thousand pounds on this play already, and there's no special reason, so far as I know, why he's keeping it running. Mary's the only woman in the cast who's worth looking at, and she's no friend of his."

"Washington Wirth? The name is familiar." Moran looked at the wall above Dick's head. "I've heard something about him or seen his name. By the way, I met an old friend of yours tonight, Surefoot Smith. You were present when that wretched man Tickler was found, weren't you?"

Dick nodded.

"The fool treated me as though I were an accomplice."

"If the fool you are referring to is Surefoot Smith, he treated me as though I were the murderer," said Dick. "Did you give him some beer?"

Leo Moran opened the door and, after looking down the deserted corridor, came back and closed the door quietly.

"I was hoping I should see you here, Dick. I want to ask you a favour."

Dick grinned.

"Nothing would give me greater joy than to refuse a favour to a bank manager," he said.

"Don't be a fool; it has nothing to do with money. Only – "

He stopped, and it seemed as if he were carefully framing his words.

"I may be out of London for a week or two. My leave is due, and I want to get into the country. I wonder if you could collect my letters at the flat and keep them for me till I come back?"

"Why not have them sent on?" said Dick, in surprise.

Leo Moran shook his head impatiently.

"I have a special reason for asking. I'm having nothing sent on at all. My servant is going away on his holiday, and the flat will be in charge of Heaven knows who. If I send you the key, will you keep an eye on the place?"

"When are you going?" asked Dick.

Moran was vague on this point; there was no certainty whether his leave would be granted. Head office was being rather difficult, although he had a most capable assistant and could have handed over at any moment.

"I want to go at once, but these brutes in the City are just being tin-godlike. You'll never know how near human beings can approach divinity until you have had dealings with general managers of banks," he said. "When you approach them you make three genuflections and stand on your head, and even then they hardly notice you! Is it a bet?"

"Surely," said Dick. "You know where to send the key. And I'll take a little cheap advice from you, now you're here."

He told him of the offer he had received for the gun. There was no need to explain what the gun was, for Leo had both seen and tested it.

"I shouldn't take an outright offer. I should prefer to take half on account of a royalty," he said, when Dick had finished. "Are you going to your flat soon?"

"Almost immediately," said the other. "Mary has a supper engagement."

"With Mr Wirth?" asked Moran with a smile.

"I thought you'd never heard of him?" said Dick.

"His name came to me as I was speaking. He's the fellow who gives these supper parties. I used to give them myself once upon a time, and Dead Sea fruit they are! But if you're going back I'll walk with you, and renew my acquaintance with your remarkable invention."

Leo Moran would have been ever so much more popular but for the fact that there was invariably a hint of sarcasm in his most commonplace remarks. Sometimes Dick, who liked him well enough, thought he had been soured by some big misfortune; for, despite his geniality, there was generally a bite to his remarks. Dick forgave him as they walked along the Strand for all that he had to say concerning Jerry Dornford.

"There's a wastrel!" said Moran. "I can't tell you why I think so, because I'm interviewing him tomorrow on bank business."

Though the evening was warm, a fog had formed, which, as their cab approached the Park, increased in density. It was clearing off as they passed through Knightsbridge.

"As a matter of fact," said Dick, "you're making me do something it has been on my conscience to do all the evening, and that is, go home and look at that gun. Like a fool, I charged it before I came out. I was about to make the experiment of trying to shoot a nickel bullet through a steel plate, and like an idiot I left it loaded. It's thicker here."

The fog was very patchy, and was so dense that the cabman had to feel his way along the kerb as they approached the house where Dick Allenby had his workshop.

The little lift was in darkness, and even when Dick turned the switch no light came. As he moved he trod on something which

54

crashed under his feet. Immediately there followed a loud and alarming explosion.

"What the devil was that?" asked Moran irritably.

Dick struck a match. He saw on the floor the remains of a small incandescent globe which had evidently been removed from the roof of the lift.

"That's odd. Our janitor is a little careless," he said, and pushed the button that sent the elevator up to the top floor. He took out a key and had another surprise, for a key was already in the lock, so tightly fitted that it could not be turned one way or the other.

He twisted the handle; the door gave.

"There's somebody been playing monkey tricks here," he said.

Turning on the light, he stood stock still, momentarily incapable of speech. The bench on which the gun had stood was empty. The gun was gone!

10

He recovered his voice at last.

"Well, I'll be...!"

Who could have taken it? He was staggered, so staggered that he could not be angry. Pulling back the door, he examined the key, and, with the aid of a pair of powerful pliers, presently extracted it. It was a rough and ready affair, badly filed, but evidently it had fitted, and had done all that its owner had required, for the lock had turned back.

It was when the unknown had tried to relock the door and take away the key that he had failed.

Dick walked to where the gun had been and glared down at the bench. Then he began to laugh.

"The brute!"

"It's a very serious loss to you, isn't it?" asked Moran.

Dick shook his head.

"Not really. All the plans and specifications are in the hands of a model-maker, and fortunately I applied for letters of patent for the main features three days ago."

He stared at Moran.

"The question is, who did it?"

And then his jaw dropped.

"If he doesn't know how to handle that thing, and isn't jolly careful, he'll either kill himself or some innocent passer-by!" he said. "I wonder if he knows how to unload it?"

He pulled out a chair and sat down, and with a gesture invited his visitor to sit.

"I suppose we ought to tell the police. Now, if old man Surefoot is at the Yard…"

He consulted an address book and gave a number.

After a long parley with a suspicious man at the Scotland Yard exchange, he found himself connected with Smith. In a few words he explained what had happened.

"I'll come up. Is there anything else missing?"

"No – the beer is intact," said Dick.

When he had hung up the receiver he went into his little larder and dragged in a wooden case.

"Surefoot will be glad; he loathes science. Don't make a face like that, my dear chap – Surefoot's clever. I used to think that beer had a deadening effect on people, but Surefoot is an amazing proof of the contrary. You don't like him?"

"I'm not passionately attached to him," said Moran. He looked at his watch. "If you don't mind, I'll leave you alone with your grief. It's hard luck – is it insured?"

"Spoken like a banker!" said Dick. "No, it isn't. Leo, I never realised I was a genius till now – it's like the things that you read about in thrillers! You see what has happened? Our friend came here in the fog, but to make absolutely sure he shouldn't be seen he took out the light in the lift, so that nobody should spot him on his way down. The door is lattice work, and if the light had been on he could have been seen from any of the floors, supposing somebody was there to see him. I presume he had a car outside; he put the gun into the machine and got away. Probably we passed him."

"Who would know you had the gun?"

Dick thought for a while.

"Mary knew; Jerry Dornford knew – By Jove!"

Leo Moran smiled and shook his head.

"Jerry wouldn't have the energy, anyway; and he wouldn't know where to market – "

He stopped suddenly.

"I saw him the other day at Snell's Club, with that poisonous little devil Jules – the fellow who is supposed to have been concerned in pinching the French mobilisation plans."

Dick hesitated, reached for the telephone directory, found the number he wanted, and put in a call. The line was engaged. Five minutes later the exchange called back to him, and he heard Jerry's voice.

"Hullo, Dornford! Got my gun?" asked Dick.

"Your what?" asked Jerry's steady voice.

"Somebody said they saw you walking out of my house with something under your arm this evening."

"I haven't seen your infernal house, and I'm not likely to see it after your beastly rudeness this afternoon!"

Click!

Jerry Dornford had hung up on him.

"I wonder," said Dick, and frowned as he slowly hung up the receiver. "I can't believe he did it, though there's nothing bad I wouldn't believe about him."

"Do you think it was your German friend?" asked Leo.

"Rubbish! Why should he offer me the money? He would have given me a draft right away this afternoon if I had wanted it. No, we'll leave it to old man Surefoot."

"Then you'll leave it to him alone," said Leo, and buttoned up his overcoat.

He went to the door and turned back.

"You'll not go back on your promise, about clearing my letters? It all depends on what happens tomorrow how soon I go, and the first intimation you'll get will be when you receive my key."

"Where are you going?" asked Dick.

Leo shook his head.

"That's the one thing I can't tell you," he said.

Sitting alone, surveying the empty bench, Dick Allenby began to realise the seriousness of his loss. If he was bewildered by the theft, the last thing in the world he expected, he was by no means shattered.

He tried to get Mary on the phone, but thought better of it. It would be selfish to spoil her night's amusement. Better start again. He was working at his drawing-board on a new plan, and had already conceived an improvement on the older model, when Surefoot Smith arrived.

He listened while Dick described the circumstances of his return; examined the key casually, and seemed more interested in the marks that the machine had made, visible against its dusty surroundings, than in anything else.

"No, it's not remarkable," he said when Dick so described the theft. "Dozens of inventions are stolen in the course of a year…yes, I mean burgled. I know a company promoter who floated a business to sell cameras, who had his house burgled and the plans of the invention stolen a week before the company was put on the market. I've known other promoters to have police guards in their houses day and night."

He walked round the room and presently related the sum of his discoveries.

"The man who took this was taller than you." He pointed to a bench near the door, the contents of which were in some disorder. "He rested the gun there while he tried to operate the lock, and that bench is higher than this. He wore gloves; he must have handled this cylinder and there's no fingerprints on it. Who has been here lately?"

Dick told him.

"Mr Gerald Dornford, eh? I shouldn't think he'd have the nerve. We had some trouble with him once; he was running a little game in the West End. I might look him up, but it would be asking for trouble. I hardly think it's worthwhile putting him under observation," said Surefoot. "Are you going to call up the Press and tell them all about it? They'll make a story of it – 'Sensational Invention Stolen. ' "

"I didn't think of doing anything so silly."

"Then you're wise," said Surefoot.

He looked helplessly around; Dick pointed to the beer case under the bench.

59

"In a way, and without any offence to you, Mr Allenby, I'm glad to see it go. All these new inventions are coming so thick and fast that you can't keep track of them."

"Which reminds me," said Dick, "that this thing was loaded."

Surefoot was not gravely concerned.

"If somebody gets shot," he said calmly, "we shall find out who did it."

He was less interested in the robbery than in the killing of Tickler.

"It's a puzzle to me. I can't understand it. I wouldn't mind if it hadn't been in that cab. It's the Americanisation of English crime that is worrying me. These Americans have got our motor-car trade, they've got our tool trade; if they come here and corner our murder market there's going to be trouble."

He stopped suddenly, stooped and picked something from the floor. It was a pearl waistcoat button.

"This sort of thing only happens in stories," he said as he turned it over. "The fellow was in evening dress, and rubbed this off when he was carrying the gun. As a clue it's about as much use as the evidence of the old lady in every murder case who saw a tall, dark man in a big, grey car."

He looked at the button carefully.

"You can buy these at almost any store in London. You don't even have to buy 'em – they give 'em away."

He made a careful scrutiny of the floor but found nothing new.

"Still, I'll put it in my pocket," he said.

"It may have been Leo Moran's," said Dick, remembering. "He wore a white waistcoat. He and I came back together."

Surefoot's nose wrinkled.

"This! It would have been diamonds and sapphires! Ain't he a bank manager? No, this is the button of some poor depositor. I shouldn't be surprised if it was somebody with an overdraft! What do you think of Mr Moran?"

He was looking at Dick keenly.

"He's a nice fellow; I like him," said Dick.

"There are moments when I don't, but, generally speaking, I do. Who's Corot?" He pronounced it as though it were spelt Corrot.

"Corot?" said Dick. "You mean the painter?"

Smith nodded.

"Oh, he's a very famous landscape artist."

"Expensive?" asked Surefoot.

"Very," said Dick. "His pictures sell for thousands."

Surefoot rubbed his nose irritably.

"That's what I thought. In fact, he said as much. Seen his flat? It looks as though it had been furnished for the Queen of Sheba, the well known Egyptian. Persian carpet, diamond lampshades…"

Dick laughed.

"You're talking about Moran's flat? Yes, it's rather beautiful. But he's got money of his own."

"It was his own when he had it, anyway," said Smith darkly, and left on this cryptic note.

He had left Scotland Yard with some reluctance, for there was visiting London at that period one John Kelly, Deputy Chief Commissioner of the Chicago Police and one of America's foremost detectives. "Great John" had been holding an audience of senior officers spellbound with stories of Chicago's gangland. Earlier in the evening Surefoot had discussed the Regent Street murder.

"It sounds like a 'ride,' " said Kelly, shaking his head, "but I guess that kind of crime will never be popular in this country. In the first place, you've no big men in your underworld, and if you had, your police force and Government are pull-proof. It reads to me like an 'imitation murder.' I suppose you've got bad men here – I only know one English gangster. They called him London Len. He was a bad egg – bumped off half a dozen men before a rival gang got after him and got him on the run. He was English-born – so far as I've been able to trace he wasn't in the country five years."

London Len was an "inside man" – he got himself into positions of trust, and at the first opportunity cleared the contents of the office safe.

"Quick on the draw and ruthless," said John; "but he certainly wouldn't give a man a hundred pounds and leave it behind when he shot him!"

Now that he was abroad on this foggy night, Surefoot decided to interview a certain forgetful constable, and before he left the Yard he arranged to meet the man at Marylebone Road station. He found the police officer in mufti, waiting in the charge room, rather proud, if anything, that he had recalled the one fact that he should not have forgotten.

Surefoot Smith listened to the story of the little man who had been found sitting on the doorstep of an apartment in Baynes Mews, and of the inebriated songster.

"It's funny I should have forgotten that – " began the policeman. "But as I was shaving this morning I thought – "

"It's not funny. If it was, I should be laughing. Am I laughing?"

"No, sir," admitted the police officer.

"It's not funny, it's tragic. If you'd been a rabbit wearing uniform, you would have remembered to tell your superior officer about that incident. A poor, harmless, lop-eared rabbit would have gone straight to his sergeant and said 'So-and-so and so-and-so.' And if a rabbit can do that, why couldn't you?"

The question was unanswerable, partly because the bewildered young constable was not sure whether "rabbit" had any special esoteric meaning.

"And you're taking credit," Surefoot went on inexorably, "for thinking – I repeat, thinking – as you were shaving this morning, that you ought to have told somebody about meeting that man in the mews. Do you use a safety razor, my man?"

"Yes, sir," said the officer.

"Then you couldn't cut your throat, which is a pity," said Surefoot. "Now lead me to this place, and don't speak unless I speak to you. I am not suspending you from duty, because I am not associated with the uniformed branch. There was a time when I was associated," he said carefully, "but in those days police constables had brains."

11

The crushed policeman led the way to Baynes Mews and pointed out the door where he had seen the figure of Tickler sitting. The door did not yield to Surefoot's pressure. He took from his pocket some skeleton keys which he had borrowed at the station without authority, and tried them on the door. Presently he so manipulated the key that he succeeded in snapping back the lock. He pushed open the door, sent a ray of light up the dusty stairs, and climbed, breathing stertorously, to the top. He came upon a landing and a barrier of matchwood, in which was a door. He tried this and again had recourse to his skeleton key.

Without a warrant he had no right whatever to invade the privacy of an English home; but Surefoot had never hesitated to break the law in the interests of justice or the satisfaction of his curiosity.

He found he was in a large, bare room, almost unfurnished except for a big, cheap-looking wardrobe, a chair, a table, a large mirror, and a square of carpet. At the back of the room, behind the matchboarding partition, was a wash-place. Singularly enough, there was no bed, not even a couch. On the wall was an old print representing the marriage of Queen Victoria. It was in a dusty maple frame and hung groggily. Mr Smith, who had a tidy mind, tried to straighten the picture, and something fell to the floor. It was a white glove which contained something heavy; it struck the floor with a clump. He picked it up and laid it on the dressing-table. The glove was of kid, with three strips of black lace at the back, and it held a key. It was nothing delicate in the way of keys, but a large, old-fashioned door-key of a type fashionable before the introduction of patent locks.

What was remarkable about this key was its colour: it had been painted with silver paint.

Surefoot looked at the key thoughtfully. An amateur had painted it – the inside of the business end had not been touched; the steel was bright and evidently the key was often used.

He brought this beneath the one naked electric globe which served to illuminate the room, but found nothing new about it. Putting the key in his pocket, he continued his search, without, however, discovering anything more noteworthy, until he found the cupboard. Its door seemed part of the matchboard lining of the room, to the height of which it rose. There was no handle, and the keyhole was so concealed in the dovetailing that it might have passed unnoticed but for the fact that Surefoot Smith was a very painstaking man.

He thought at first it was a Yale lock, but when he tested it out with the aid of a big clasp-knife, which contained half a dozen tools, he found it was a very simple "catch." The cupboard held a complete dress suit, including silk hat and overcoat. On a shelf was a number of plain but exquisitely woven handkerchiefs, socks, folded dress ties and the like.

He searched the pockets but could find no clue to the ownership of the suit. There was no maker's tab on the inside of the coat, or concealed in the breast pocket. Even the trousers buttons were not inscribed with the tailor's name.

He examined the dress shirts; they were similarly unidentifiable. He found nothing more except a large bottle of expensive perfume, a monocle attached to a broad silk ribbon, and a locked box. This he forced under the lamp, and found three wigs, perfectly made. One was wrapped in silver tissue, and it was either new or had been newly dressed.

"Bit queer, isn't it?" said Surefoot Smith aloud.

"Yes, sir," said the constable, who had been silent until that moment.

"I was talking to myself," said Surefoot coldly. He made another round of the room, but without adding to the sum of his knowledge.

He replaced everything where he had found it, except the key and the glove. After all, there might be a perfectly simple explanation of his finds. The man may have been an actor. The fact that Tickler had been sitting on his doorstep, listening to his drunken song, meant little, and would certainly carry no weight with a jury.

On the other hand, if the explanation was so simple, Surefoot Smith was in a position of some embarrassment. Against his name, if the truth be told, were many black marks for unauthorised entry. This might very well be the cause of another.

He went out into the mews, locked the door, and walked silently into Portland Place, followed by the policeman. And Surefoot Smith did not forget that the constable might possibly be a witness at any inquiry before the Commissioner.

"I think that is all, officer," he said, "but I am not blaming you for failing to report. Things like that," he went on, "slip out of a man's mind. For instance, I left my house yesterday and forgot to take my pipe."

The officer murmured his polite surprise. He was a little mollified, and was sufficiently intelligent to understand the reason for this change of attitude.

"I suppose it's all right, sir, going into that place without a warrant?" he said. "I'm asking because I'm a young officer, new to the force – "

Surefoot Smith surveyed him soberly.

"I went," he said, with great deliberation, "because you reported a suspicious circumstance. You told me you had reason to believe that the murderer might be hiding in that loft."

The constable gasped at this atrocious charge, gasped but was speechless.

"So that, if there's any trouble over it," said Surefoot, "we're both in it. And my word's better than yours. Now go home and keep your mouth shut – it won't be hard for you." He could not resist the temptation to gibe. "In fact, I should say you were a pretty good mouth-shutter."

The key and the white glove he locked away in a drawer of his desk at Scotland Yard. There was nothing remarkable about either article. Surefoot Smith would indeed have been glad to sacrifice his finds for one packet of cartridges, the bullets of which corresponded to those extracted from the unfortunate Tickler. In his mind, however, he was satisfied that there was some connection between that flat in Baynes Mews and the murder of the little thief. The finding of the dress clothes signified little; it might only mean that some swell, for reasons best known to himself, wanted a place where he could change without going home. Such things happen in the West End of London, and in the east or any other end of any other large city.

The absence of the bed rather puzzled him, but here again it simply removed one explanation of the flat being used. Yet, if he could have foreseen the future, he would have known that he had in his possession a clue more valuable than the science of ballistics could have given to him.

12

Mary Lane's party was a very dull one. She was one of ten young people, and young people can be very boring. Three of the girls had a giggling secret, and throughout the meal made esoteric references to some happening which none but they understood. The young men were vapid and vacuous, after their kind. She was glad to get away on the excuse of a matinée.

Mary lived in a large block of flats in the Marylebone Road. These three small rooms and a kitchenette were home and independence to her. She seldom received visitors, rarely men visitors, and never in any circumstances invited a guest so late at night. She was staggered when the lift-man told her that "a gentleman had just gone up to her flat."

"No, miss, I've never seen him before. It wasn't Mr Allenby, but he says he knows you."

He opened the door of the lift and walked along the corridor with her. To her amazement she saw Leo Moran, who had evidently rung the bell of the flat several times, and was returning to the elevator when they met.

"It is unpardonable of me to come so late, Miss Lane, but when I explain to you that it's rather a vital matter I'm sure you will not be angry with me. Your maid is asleep."

Mary smiled.

"I haven't a maid," she said.

The situation was a little embarrassing: she could hardly ask him into the flat; still less did she find it possible to suggest that the lift-man should be her chaperon. She compromised by asking him in and leaving the front door open.

Moran was nervous; his voice, when he spoke, was husky; the hand that took a large envelope from his inside pocket was unsteady.

"I wouldn't have bothered you at all, but I had rather a discon-certing letter when I got home, from – an agent of mine."

She knew Moran, though she had never regarded him as a friend, and felt a sense of resentment every time he had come unbidden to her dressing-room. Since she received her allowance from old Hervey, she had it also through the bank of which Leo Moran was manager.

"I'll be perfectly frank with you, Miss Lane," he said, speaking quickly and nervously. "It's a matter entirely personal to myself, in the sense that I am personally responsible. The one man who could get me out of my trouble is the one man I do not wish to approach – your guardian, Mr Hervey Lyne."

To say she was astonished is to put it mildly. She had always regarded Moran as a man so perfectly self-possessed that nothing could break through his reserve, and here he was, fidgeting and stammering like a schoolboy.

"If I can help you of course I will," she said, wondering what was coming next.

"It concerns some shares which I purchased on behalf of a client of the bank. Mr Lyne signed the transfer, but the other people – that is to say, the people to whom the shares were transferred – have just discovered that it is necessary also that your name shall be on the transfer, as they originally were part of the stocks left in trust to you. I might say," he went on quickly, "that the price of this stock is exactly the same, or practically the same, as it was when it was taken over."

"My name – is that all you want? I thought at least it was something valuable," she laughed.

He put the paper on the table; it was indubitably a stock transfer; she had seen such documents before. He indicated where her name should be signed, and she noticed above it the scrawl of old Lyne.

"Well, that's done."

There was no mistaking his relief.

"You'll think I'm an awful brute to come at this hour of the night. I can't tell you how grateful I am. It simply meant that I had paid out money of the bank's without the necessary authorisation. Also, if old Mr Lyne died tomorrow, this transfer would be practically valueless."

She made a little grimace.

"Is he likely to die tomorrow?"

He shook his head.

"I don't know; he's a pretty old man."

Abruptly he held out his hand.

"Goodnight, and thank you again."

She closed the door on him, went back to her kitchenette to make herself a cup of chocolate before she went to bed, and sat for a long time at the kitchen table, sipping the hot decoction, and trying to discover something sinister in his midnight visitation. Herein she failed. If Hervey Lyne died tomorrow? By his agitation and hurry one might imagine that the old man was in extremis. Yet, the last time she had seen old Hervey, he was very much in possession of his faculties.

She was at breakfast the following morning when Dick Allenby called her up and told her of his loss. She listened incredulously, and thought he was joking until he told her of the visit of Surefoot Smith.

"My dear – how terrible!" she said.

"Surefoot thought it was providential. Moran thought nothing."

"Was he there?" she asked quickly.

"Yes – why?"

She hesitated. Moran had so evidently wished his visit to her to be a private matter that it seemed like betraying him.

"Oh, nothing," she said. And then, as an afterthought: "Come round and tell me all about it."

He was there in half an hour, singularly unemotional and cheerful, she thought.

"It really isn't as dramatically important as it sounds," he said. "If it has been stolen, as Surefoot thinks it has, with the idea of pinching the patent, the buyer will be shrewd enough to make a search of the registrations at the various Patent Offices. I had an acknowledgment from Germany this morning that it has been entered there."

He was interrupted by a knock at the outer door and she opened it to admit a second visitor. It was not usual, she explained apologetically to Dick, that she should receive guests so early, but Mike Hennessey had telephoned, asking whether he might come.

The first thing she noticed when Mike came into the room was his embarrassment at finding Dick Allenby there. A genial soul was Mike, big-faced, heavy-featured, sleepy-eyed, constitutionally lazy and lethargic in his movements. He was never a healthy-looking individual, but now he looked positively ill, and she remarked upon the fact. Mike shook his head.

"Had a bad night," he said. "Good morning, Mr Allenby – don't go: I've nothing private; only I wanted to see this young lady about our play. It's coming off."

"Thank Heaven for that!" said Mary gratefully. "It's the best news I've had for months."

"It's about the worst I've had," he grumbled.

"Has Mr Wirth withdrawn his support?"

It was nearer the truth than she guessed. Mr Wirth's weekly cheque, which had been due on the previous day, had not arrived, and Mike was taking no chances.

"The notice goes up tonight that we finish on Saturday," he said. "I've had the luck to let the theatre – I wish I'd taken a better offer that I had last week."

He was even more nervous than Moran had been; could not keep his hands still or his body either. He got up from the chair, walked to the window, came back and sat down, only to rise again a few moments later.

"Who is this old fellow Wirth? What's his job?" asked Dick.

"I don't know. He's in some sort of business at Coventry," said Mike. "I thought of running up there today to see him. The point is this" – he came to that point bluntly – "tomorrow night's Treasury, and I haven't enough money in the bank to pay the artistes. I may get it today, in which case there's no fuss. You're the heaviest salary in the cast, Mary: will you trust me till next week if things go wrong?"

She was staggered at the suggestion. In the case of other productions Mike's solvency had always been a matter of the gravest doubt, but *Cliffs of Fate* had been under more distinguished patronage, and the general impression was that, whatever else happened, the money for its continuance would come in.

"Of course I will, Mike," she said; "but surely Mr Wirth hasn't – "

"Gone broke? No, I shouldn't think so. He's a queer man," said Mike vaguely.

He did not particularise his patron's queerness, but was satisfied to leave it at that. His departure was almost as abrupt a gesture as any he had performed.

"There's a pretty sick man," said Dick.

"Do you mean he's ill?"

"Mentally. Something's upset him. I should imagine that the failure of old Wirth's cheque was quite sufficient; but there's something else besides."

He rose.

"Come and lunch," he invited, but she shook her head.

She was lunching at home; her matinée excuse at the overnight party had been on the spur of the moment. She wondered how many would remember it against her.

Dick went on to Scotland Yard, and had to wait half an hour before Surefoot Smith returned. He had no news of any importance. A description of the stolen gun had been circulated.

"But that won't help you very much. It's hardly likely to be pawned or offered for sale in the Caledonian Market," said Surefoot. And then, abruptly: "Do you know Mr Washington Wirth?"

"I've heard of him."

"Have you ever met him? Great party giver, isn't he?"

Dick smiled.

"He's never given me a party, but I believe he is rather keen on that sort of amusement."

Surefoot nodded.

"I've just been up to the Kellner Hotel. They know nothing about him except that he always pays in cash. He's been using the hotel for three years; orders a suite whenever he feels inclined, leaves the supper and the band to the head waiter; but that's the only thing they know about him – that his money is good money, which is all they want to know, I suppose."

"Are you interested in him?" asked Dick, and told the story of Mike Hennessey's agitation.

Surefoot Smith was interested.

"He's got a bank, has he? Well, he may be one of those Midland people. I've never understood what makes the corn and coal merchants go in for theatricals. It's a form of insanity that's been pretty common since the war."

"Mike will tell you all about it," suggested Allenby.

Mr Smith's lips curled.

"Mike'll tell us a whole lot," he said sarcastically. "That fellow wouldn't tell you his right hand had four fingers, for fear you brought it up in evidence against him. I know Mike!"

"At any rate, he's got a line on Wirth," said Dick. "He's been financing this play."

Since he could find nobody to lunch with, he decided to take that meal at Snell's, which had all the values of a good club except that there were one or two members who were personally objectionable to him. And the most poisonous were the first two he saw at the entrance of the dining-room. Gerald Dornford and Jules had their little table in the window. Jules favoured him with a nod, but Jerry kept his eyes steadily averted as Dick passed.

They had, in point of fact, only just sat down when Allenby had arrived, and in his furtive way Jules had been avoiding the one subject which his companion wished to discuss. He spoke of the people who were passing in the street, recognising every important motor-car that passed; he talked of the military conference which was in session just then, of the party to which he had been the night before, of anything but –

"Now what about this gun?" said Jerry.

"The gun?"

Jules looked at him blankly, then leaned back in his chair and chuckled.

"What a good thing you came today! I wanted to see you. That little project of mine must be abandoned."

"What do you mean?" gasped Jerry, turning pale.

"I mean that my principals, or rather the principals of my principals, have decided not to go any farther in the matter. You see, we've discovered that all the salient points of the gun have been protected by patents, especially in those countries where the invention could be best exploited."

Jerry looked at him, dumbfounded.

"Do you mean to say that you don't want it?"

Jules nodded.

"I mean to say that there's no need for you to take any unnecessary risks. Now let us discuss some other way of raising the money."

"Discuss be damned!" said Jerry savagely. "I've got the gun – I took it last night!"

Jules stroked his smooth chin and looked at his companion thoughtfully.

"That's awkward," he said. "You took it from the workshop, did you? Well, you can hardly put it back. I advise you to drive somewhere out of London and dump it in a deep pond. Or, better still, try the river, somewhere between Temple Lock and Hambleden."

"Do you mean to tell me" – Jerry's husky voice was almost hoarse – "that I've taken this risk for nothing? What is the idea?"

Jules shrugged.

"I'm sorry. My principals – "

"Damn your principals! You gave me a specific promise that if I got the thing you'd give me a couple of thousand."

Jules smiled.

"And now, my dear fellow, I give you a specific assurance that I cannot get two thousand shillings for the gun! It is unfortunate. If you had procured the invention when I first suggested it, the matter would have been all over – and paid for. Now it is too late."

He leaned over and patted the other gently on the arm as though he were a child.

"There is no sense in being foolish about this matter," he said. "Let us find some other way of raising the wind, eh?"

Jerry Dornford was crushed. He knew Hervey Lyne sufficiently well to realise that, had he produced the two thousand pounds, the old man would have grabbed at the money and given him the extra time he had asked. Hervey could never resist the argument of cash.

He could have grabbed the smiling little cad opposite him and thrown him out of the window. There was murder in his glance when he looked into the round, brown eyes of his companion. But Jerry Dornford never forgot he was a gentleman, and as such was expected to exercise the self-control which is the peculiar and popular attribute of the well bred man.

"Well, it can't be helped," he said. "Order me a drink; I'm a bit rattled."

Jules played an invisible piano on the edge of the table.

"Our friend Allenby is at the third table on the right. Would it not be a good idea," he suggested, "to go over and say: 'What a little joke I played on you, eh?'"

"Don't be a fool," interrupted Jerry roughly. "He called me up last night and asked me if I had it. He's put the matter in the hands of the police. I had a visit from Smith this morning."

"So!" Jules pursed his red lips. "That is a pity. Here is your drink."

They sat for a long time over their coffee, saw Dick Allenby leave the club and cross to the opposite side of St James's Street.

"Clever fellow, that," said Jules, almost with enthusiasm. "He doesn't like me. I forget the name he called me the last time we had a little discussion, but it was terribly offensive. But I like him. I am fond of clever people; there is nothing so amusing as cleverness."

Dick had hardly left the club before a telephone message came through for him, and this he missed. It was Mary Lane, and at that moment she needed Dick's advice very badly. She called his flat again; he had not returned. She tried a third club, where he sometimes called in the afternoon, but again was unsuccessful.

She had been writing out the small cheques which her housekeeping necessitated, when the strange message had arrived. It came in the hands of a grubby little boy, who carried an envelope which was covered with uncleanly fingermarks.

"An old gentleman told me to bring it here," he said in his shrill Cockney.

An old gentleman? She looked at the superscription; her name and address were scrawled untidily, and although she had not seen Hervey Lyne's handwriting, she knew, or rather guessed, that it was he who had sent the letter.

The boy explained that he had been delivering a parcel at No.19, and had seen the old gentleman leaning on his stick in the doorway. He wore his dressing-gown and had the letter in his hand. He had called the boy, given him half a crown (that must have been a wrench for Hervey), and ordered him to deliver the letter at once.

She tore it open. It was written on the back of a ruled sheet of paper covered with typewritten figures, and the writing was in pencil.

"Bring Moran to me without fail at three o'clock this afternoon. I saw him two days ago, but I'm not satisfied. Bring police officer."

Here was written, above, a word which she deciphered as "Smith."

"Do not let Moran or anybody know about PO. This is very urgent."

The note was signed "H L."

The little boy could give her no other information. She would have called up Mr Lyne's house, but the old man had an insuperable objection to the telephone and had never had one installed. She looked at her watch; it was after two, and for ten minutes she was making a frantic effort to get in touch with Dick.

Surefoot Smith she hardly knew well enough to consult, and she had a woman's distaste for approaching the police direct. She called up Mr Moran's bank; he had gone home. She tried his club, with no better success. Moran had left his flat that morning, announcing that he had no intention of returning for two or three weeks. He had gone on leave. Curiously enough, the bank did not tell her that: they merely said that Mr Moran had gone home early – a completely inaccurate piece of information, she discovered when the first man, who was evidently a clerk, was interrupted and a more authoritative voice spoke: "This is the chief accountant speaking, Miss Lane. You were asking about Mr Moran? He has not been to the bank today."

"He's gone on leave, hasn't he?"

"I'm not aware of the fact. I know he has applied for leave, but I don't think he's gone – in fact, I'm certain. I opened all the letters this morning."

She hung up the telephone, bewildered, and was sitting at the window, cogitating on what else she should do, when to her joy the telephone rang. It was Dick, who had returned to Snell's Club to collect some letters he had forgotten, and had been told of her call.

"That's very odd," was his comment when he heard about the note. "I'll try to get Smith. The best thing you can do, angel, is to meet me outside Baker Street Tube Station in a quarter of an hour. I'll try to land Smith at the same moment."

She got to the station a little before three, and had to wait for ten minutes before a taxicab dashed up and Dick jumped out. She saw the bulky figure of Mr Smith in one corner of the cab, and, getting in, sat by him. Dick gave instructions to the taxi driver and seated himself opposite.

"This is all very mysterious, isn't it?" he said. "Let me see the letter."

She showed it to him, and he turned it over.

"Hullo, this is a bank statement." He whistled. "Phew! What figures! The old boy's certainly let the cat out of the bag."

She had paid no attention to the typewritten statement on the back.

"Over two hundred thousand in cash and umpteen hundred thousand in securities. What is the idea – I mean, of sending this note? I suppose you couldn't find Moran?"

She shook her head.

Smith was examining the letter carefully.

"Is he blind?" he asked.

"Very nearly," said Dick. "He doesn't admit it, but he can't see well enough to distinguish you from me. That's his writing – I had a rude letter from him one day last week. Did you find Moran?"

Mary shook her head.

"Nobody seems to know where he is. He hasn't been to the bank today, and he's not at his flat."

Surefoot folded the letter and handed it back to the girl.

"It looks as if he doesn't want to see me yet awhile, and not at all if we don't bring Moran," he said.

They drove into Naylors Crescent, and it was agreed that Surefoot should sit outside in the cab whilst they interviewed the old man. But repeated knockings brought no answer. The houses in Naylors Crescent stand behind deep little areas, and out of one of these next door a head appeared.

"There's nobody in," he said. "Mr Lyne has gone out in his chair about an hour ago."

"Where did he go?" asked Dick.

The servant could not say; but Mary was better informed.

"They always go to the same place – into the private gardens of the park," she said. "It's only a few minutes' walk."

The cab was no longer necessary; Dick paid it off. They were about to cross the road when a big, open touring car swept past, and Dick had a momentary glimpse of the man at the wheel. It was Jerry Dornford. The car was old and noisy; there was a succession of backfires as it passed. It slowed down a little at one point, then, gathering speed, disappeared from view.

"Any policeman doing his duty will pinch that fellow under the Noises Act," said Smith.

Presently they came in sight of the chair. Binny was sitting on his little collapsible stool, a paper spread open on his knees, a pair of gold-rimmed glasses perched on his thick nose. The gate into the gardens was locked and it was some time before Dick attracted the servant's attention. Presently Binny looked up, and, ambling forward, unlocked the gate and admitted them.

"I think he's asleep, sir," he said, "and that's a bit awkward. If I start wheeling him when he's asleep, and he wakes up, he gives me hell! And he's got to be home by three."

Old Hervey Lyne sat, his chin on his breast, his blue-tinted glasses firmly fixed on the high bridge of his nose. His gloved hands were clasped on the rug which was tucked about his legs, Binny folded his paper, put it in his pocket, folded his stool and hung it on a little hook on the bath-chair.

"Do you think you'd better wake him up?"

Mary went nearer.

"Mr Lyne," she said.

She called again, but there was no answer.

Surefoot Smith, who was standing at some distance, came nearer. He walked round the back of the chair, came to the front, and, leaning over, pulled open the old man's coat. He closed it again; then, to Mary's amazement, Surefoot Smith caught her gently by the arm.

"I think you'd better run away for about an hour, and I'll come and see you at your flat," he said.

His voice was unusually gentle.

She looked at him, and the colour went out of her face.

"Is he dead?" she breathed.

Surefoot Smith nodded; almost impelled her towards the gate. When she was out of hearing: "He's been shot through the back. I saw the hole in the cape as I came round. Look!" He opened the coat.

Dick saw something that was not pleasant to see.

13

The ambulance had come and gone. Four men sat in the dead man's study. Binny was one; the other, besides Surefoot Smith and Dick Allenby, was the divisional inspector.

Smith turned to the grey-faced servant.

"Tell us just what happened, my boy," he said.

Binny shook his head.

"I don't know…awful, ain't it, him going like that…"

"Were there any visitors?"

Binny shook his head again.

"Nobody, so far as I know."

"Where was he at one o'clock?"

"In this room, sir, in the chair where you're sitting," said Binny. "He was writing something – put his hand over it when I came in. I didn't see what it was."

"It was probably a letter to Miss Lane," said the detective. "Does he often write notes?"

Binny shook his head.

"When he does write them do you deliver them?"

Binny shook his head again.

"No, sir, not always. Poor Mr Lyne was very suspicious. His sight wasn't very good and he'd got an idea that people was listening at the door or reading his letters. He'd call anybody off the street to take a note when he sent one, which wasn't often."

"What visitors has he had lately?"

"Mr Dornford came last night, sir. There was a bit of a quarrel – over money, I think."

"A bad quarrel?" asked Smith.

Binny nodded.

"He asked me to throw him out – Mr Lyne did."

Surefoot jotted down a note.

"And who else?"

Binny looked serious.

"Mr Moran came two days ago."

"That's right, sir. Mr Moran came to see him about banking business, and Miss Lane came – I think that's the lot. We don't often have people call."

Again Smith scribbled something. He employed a weird kind of shorthand, which was indecipherable to Dick, who, from where he sat, had a view of the notes.

"Tell us what happened today. Do you usually go out in the afternoon?"

"Yes, sir, but at lunchtime Mr Lyne said he wouldn't go out. In fact, he told me not to bother about the chair, that he was expecting some visitors at three o'clock. About two o'clock he changed his mind and said he'd go out. I pulled him into the park gardens and sat down and read a case to him – "

"Do you mean a police court case?"

"That's right, sir. He likes reading about moneylenders' actions against people who owe them something. There was a case this morning – "

"Oh, you mean a Law Courts case – any kind of case, in fact?"

Binny nodded.

"Did he say anything in the park?"

"Nothing at all, sir, of any consequence. He'd been sitting there a quarter of an hour and he asked me to turn up the collar of his coat; he was feeling a draught. I sat down and read to him until I thought he was asleep."

"You heard no sound?"

He thought a moment.

"Yes, there was a bit of a noise, from a car that went past."

For a moment both Smith and Dick had forgotten Gerald Dornford's car, and they exchanged a glance.

"You heard nothing like a shot?"

Binny shook his head.

"Nothing more than the motor-car noise," he said.

"Did Mr Lyne speak at all – groan, move?"

"No, sir."

Surefoot settled his elbows on the table.

"This is the question I want to ask you, Binny: How long before we found Mr Lyne was dead did you hear him speak?"

Binny considered.

"About ten minutes, sir," he said. "A park keeper came along and said good afternoon to him, and, when he didn't answer, I thought he was asleep. That's when I stopped reading."

"Now show me the house," said Smith, rising.

Binny led the way, first to the kitchen, from which opened a bedroom.

His wife was away in the country, living with relations, he told Surefoot, but that made little difference to Lyne's comfort, for Binny did most of the work.

"To tell you the truth, sir, my wife drinks," he said apologetically, "and I'm glad to have her out of the house."

The kitchen was none too tidy. Surefoot Smith saw something on the floor, stooped and picked up a triangular piece of glass from under the table beneath the window. He looked up at the window, felt the puttied edge.

"Had a window broken in?"

Binny hesitated.

"Mr Lyne didn't want to say anything about it. Somebody broke the glass and opened the window a couple of nights ago."

"A burglar?"

"Mr Lyne thought it was somebody trying to get in. I didn't send for the police, because he wouldn't let me," he hastened to exculpate himself.

They went upstairs to the front room. There was only one large room on each floor, though both could be divided into two by folding doors. The top room had been Lyne's bedroom, but presented no particular features. A divisional inspector and two of his men would conduct a leisurely search through the possessions and papers of the dead man – Surefoot had taken the keys from the old man's pocket. He had already made a casual inspection of the safe without discovering anything of moment.

They came back to the study. Surefoot Smith stood for a long time, staring out of the window, drumming his fingers on the leather covered top of the desk. When he spoke it was half to himself.

"There's an American going back to New York tomorrow who might tell us something. I've a good mind to bring him down to a consultation."

"Who's that?" asked Dick curiously.

"John Kelly – he's chief of the detective force in Chicago. He might give us an angle, and then again he mightn't. It's worth trying."

He looked at his watch.

"I wonder if there's any news of Moran – I'm going to look at his flat. I suppose there'll be a servant there?"

"If there isn't," said Dick, "I can help you. He told me he was going away and that he intended sending me the key, so that I could forward any letters that arrived. If you don't mind I'll walk round with you."

The housekeeper of the flat gave a surprising piece of information. Mr Moran had left only an hour before.

"Are you sure?" asked Dick incredulously. "Didn't he leave this morning?"

The man was very emphatic.

"No, sir, he's been out all the morning, but he didn't actually leave till about half-past three. You're Mr Allenby, aren't you?" He addressed Dick. "I've got a letter to post for you."

He went to his little office, came out, opened the post-box and took out a stamped envelope which contained a few lines, evidently written in a hurry, and the key of the flat.

"I'm just off. Those brutes have turned me down."

"Who are the brutes?" asked Surefoot.

Dick smiled.

"I presume he's referring to his directors. He told me he was going on his holiday whether they agreed or not."

When they entered the flat there was evidence of Moran's hurried departure. They found, for example, a waistcoat hanging from the edge of the bed, in which was his watch and chain, a gold cigarette case, and about ten pounds in cash. He had evidently changed his clothes quickly and had forgotten to empty his pockets. Another peculiar fact, which both Surefoot and Dick remarked, was that the window overlooking the park had been left open.

"Do you notice anything?" asked Surefoot.

Dick nodded, and a little chill went down his spine. From where he stood, by the open window, he commanded a view, not only of the private gardens, but of the actual spot where old Hervey Lyne had been killed.

Surefoot searched the floor near the window but found nothing. He passed into Moran's elegant bedroom and made a rapid search. Pulling out the wardrobe door, something fell out. He had time to catch it before it reached the floor. It was a Lee-Enfield rifle; a second lay flat on the wardrobe floor, and, near it, half a dozen long black cylinders.

Surefoot snapped open the breech and smelt. He had taken the rifle to the window; he placed the block upon the sill and squinted down the barrel.

If it had been recently fired then it must have been recently cleaned, for there was no sign of fouling. He tested the other rifle in the same way; and then he took up one of the cylinders.

"What are those?" he said.

Dick looked at them carefully.

"They're silencers," he said. "But Moran is very much interested in rifle shooting, especially in any new brand of silencer. He has consulted me once or twice, and has frequently urged me to take up the making of silencers. You mustn't forget, Smith, that Mr Moran is an enthusiastic rifleman. In fact, he's been runner-up for the King's Prize at Bisley, and shooting was about his only recreation."

"And a pretty good recreation too," said Smith dryly.

He searched the wardrobe and the drawers for cartridges, but could find none. The magazines of both rifles were empty. There was no sign of a discharged shell anywhere in the flat.

Smith went back to the window and judged the distance which separated the room from the place of the killing.

"Less than two hundred yards," he suggested, and Dick Allenby agreed.

Moran had not taken his servant. Surefoot got his address from the housekeeper and wired him to report at once.

"You'd better go along and see the young lady. She's probably having hysterics by now – "

"It's hardly likely," said Dick coldly, "but I'll see her. Where are you going?"

Surefoot smiled mysteriously; though why he should make a mystery of the most obvious move, it was hard to say.

14

The bank premises were closed when he reached them; he rang a bell at the side door and was admitted. The accountant and the chief clerk and two or three other clerks were on duty. He interviewed the accountant in his office.

"I know nothing whatever about Mr Moran's movements except that he applied for leave and it was not granted. I know that, because the letter from the head office did not come addressed to him personally, but to 'the manager,' and was opened by me. I got him on the phone and told him; he said nothing except that he wouldn't be down today."

"Have you reported this to your head office?" asked Surefoot.

No report had been made. It was not a very extraordinary happening. Bank managers do occasionally decide to stay away from business; and, as it happened, there had been no enquiries by phone from headquarters, and the fact had not been mentioned.

"It will go in, of course, in the daily report," said the accountant. "To tell you the truth, I was under the impression that Mr Moran had gone up to the City and had interviewed the managing director; so that when I heard he was taking his leave I naturally supposed that he had persuaded the head office to change its mind. Has anything happened to Mr Moran?" he asked anxiously.

"I hope not, I'm sure," said Smith with spurious solicitude. "Did he bank with you?"

"He had an account at this branch, but carried only a small balance," explained the accountant. "There was a little trouble about speculation a few years back, and naturally, I suppose, Mr Moran did not run his main account through us, not wishing the directors to know his business. I can tell you for your private information that he banks with the Southern Provincial. I know that, because once, when his account with us was low, he paid in a cheque on that bank to put it in credit. May I ask, Mr Smith, what is the reason for this enquiry?"

In a few words Surefoot told him of the murder.

"Yes, we carry Mr Lyne's account. It is a fairly large one – not as large as it used to be – he is a moneylender and has a lot of money out."

Smith looked at his watch.

"Is it possible to see any of the directors at headquarters?"

The accountant was doubtful, but he put through a telephone call, only to return with the information that all the directors had gone home.

"If Mr Moran doesn't turn up in the morning – "

"He won't," said Surefoot.

"Well, if he doesn't, I'd be glad if you saw the head office. I really ought not to be giving you any kind of information, either about Mr Moran or about any of our customers. Just one moment."

He went behind a desk and consulted a clerk. After a while he came back.

"I might tell you this, whether I get into trouble or not, that the late Mr Lyne drew sixty thousand pounds from the bank yesterday – that is to say, the cheque came into us and was cleared last night. It was a bearer cheque and passed through some bank in the Midlands. I can't give you the exact details, but I've no doubt head office will give you the authorisation."

When Surefoot returned to Scotland Yard he found a group of officers in his room. They were saying goodbye to John Kelly, who was leaving at midnight for the United States.

"I'm sorry," he said, when he heard Surefoot's idea. "Nothing would have given me greater pleasure than to have got in on a murder case. I read it in the evening papers. Have there been any developments?"

Surefoot told him what he had learned at the bank and the American nodded.

"You might do worse than look after a man called Arthur Ryan," he said. "I know that he's in England – I'll send you some photographs of him taken when I was in Chicago. That was part of his graft, running banking accounts, switching somebody else's money from one to the other. You'd never guess he was that kind of bird."

Surefoot was forced to resign, with regret, the invitation to an informal farewell dinner. The Chief Constable was waiting for him, a little impatiently, for his dinner hour was more formal.

"We'll have to circulate a description of Moran," said the chief when he had finished, "but it must be done without publicity, or we'll be getting ourselves into all sorts of trouble. The fact that he keeps a couple of rifles in his room means nothing. Even I know him as a rifle shot. So far as we are aware, there is nothing wrong at the bank, and the only circumstance connecting him with the crime is the old man's note. Have you got it?"

Mary had handed the note to the detective, who produced it from his pocket and spread it on the table.

The Chief Constable nodded.

"The fact that he wants to see Moran again – had he seen him before?"

"Two days ago, according to Binny, the servant – not for two years, according to Moran," said Surefoot slowly, and the Chief looked up.

"Moran said he hadn't seen – "

Surefoot nodded.

"That's just what he said. Allenby asked him casually the night before the murder when he had seen Lyne last. He said two years ago. Allenby is absolutely definite. Now, why did he say he hadn't seen him when he had? And why did old Lyne, when he sent that note, say 'Bring Moran' and immediately follow this by asking for a police officer to be in attendance? There's only one explanation – that he'd discovered something about Moran and intended either to confront him or threaten him with police action. Moran applies for urgent leave from the bank, and this isn't granted. He doesn't come to the bank, and I think we'll find, when I make enquiries at their head office, that the directors know nothing about his being away. Moran had the handling of the old man's account, and if there was anything wrong it meant penal servitude for him; probably the only person who could say whether anything was wrong was Lyne himself. He dies – somebody puts a bullet in him – half an hour before Moran leaves London. That's circumstantial, but better circumstantial evidence than most people are hung on. If you want anything clearer than that, lead me to it."

He continued his enquiries throughout the evening, and about a quarter of an hour before the curtain came down – the penultimate curtain, as it proved – on *Cliffs of Fate*, he called at the theatre. Mike Hennessey had gone home, as his manager dramatically described, "a broken man."

"He'd set his heart on this play, Mr Smith – " began the little manager, but Surefoot silenced him.

"Nobody could set their hearts on a lousy play like this," he said. "It doesn't appeal either to the intelligent or the theatrical classes."

He went through the pass door to the stage, and down a long corridor to Mary's dressing-room. Dick Allenby, as he had expected, was with her. She looked tired; evidently the old man's death had been a greater shock to her than either Dick or Surefoot Smith could have expected.

"Oh yes, the play comes off; but things aren't so bad with poor Mike as he expected. His cheque turned up and he was able to pay the company, and, I hope, himself."

She could tell him nothing about Hervey Lyne, but she was very informative about Leo Moran when he began to question her. He heard the story of his midnight call – it was news to Dick also.

"But, my dear, I don't understand. He wanted you to sign a transfer – "

"Did you notice the name of the shares?" interrupted Surefoot.

This she had not seen. Surefoot, who knew a great deal about the City and had been in many financial cases, suggested that it must be a foreign stock. It is the rule on certain foreign Stock Exchanges that shares cannot be transferred by a trustee without the approval and signature of the beneficiaries for whom he is acting.

"There is nothing fishy about that," said Surefoot thoughtfully. "Even if he was a buyer, old Lyne would not have put his name to a transfer unless he had his money's worth."

Surefoot could do little more that night. Lyne's documents were being carefully examined and tabulated, and the place of the murder was roped off and guarded, a precautionary measure justified when, at midnight, the surgeon's report came through.

Hervey Lyne had been killed by a bullet which passed through his heart from behind. Actually no bullet was found in the body, and Surefoot gave orders that at daybreak every inch of the lawn where the murder was committed should be searched for the spent bullet. By nine o'clock he was in the City, awaiting the arrival of the great men of the bank. As he had expected, no leave had been granted to Leo Moran, against whose name there was a black mark in the bank's books.

"He was a very capable manager, and very popular with our clients; otherwise, I doubt if we should have kept him after his speculations. We know nothing against him whatever, except, of course, this act of indiscipline."

"If he's gone away he has simply taken French leave?" asked Surefoot.

"Exactly," said the managing director, "and that is a very serious offence. We believe he is in Devonshire – at least, that is where he said he was going."

Surefoot smiled.

"He's not in Devonshire – I can tell you that," he said. "He left by a specially chartered aeroplane from Croydon at twenty minutes past four yesterday afternoon for Cologne. Another plane was waiting to take him to Berlin, and there we have not as yet traced him."

The managing director looked at him open-mouthed. Surefoot thought he turned a little pale.

"In Berlin?"

He could hardly believe it. One could almost see his mind working. Leo Moran's branch carried very heavy accounts, and a branch manager who disappears suddenly, and in suspicious circumstances, might not have gone empty-handed.

"I shouldn't imagine anything is wrong." He was very much perturbed. "Beyond the fact that he speculated – and, of course, one never knows to what length a gambler will go – he was a very honest, high-principled man. He had, I know, dreams of making a great fortune, but then we have all passed through that stage without doing anything dishonest."

He pressed a bell.

"Nevertheless, I will have an immediate examination of the books, and will send down our two best inspectors. We must replace Mr Moran at once."

Surefoot had managed to get a very accurate description of Leo Moran, but could find no photograph of him. He should not be difficult to trace; he was almost completely bald, which fact, however, he could disguise, if he had reason for disguise at all, with a wig –

Surefoot stopped in his reasoning and frowned. A wig! He remembered the three wigs he had found in a little room over the garage in Baynes Mews; and he recalled, too, the name of Mr Washington Wirth who lived in the Midlands… Sixty thousand pounds had gone from Lyne's account on the previous day through a Midland branch bank.

He asked for and secured authority for obtaining complete information regarding any account that was in Moran's branch, and, armed with this, he went back to the bank and interviewed the chief accountant.

"I happen to know the state of Mr Lyne's account up till a few days ago," he said. "By error he wrote a note to his ward on the back of the statement."

He produced it from his pocket, and the accountant examined it.

"I'll just check this up," he said. "This would not, of course, show the sixty thousand pounds which was debited the day before yesterday."

He was gone a long time, then came back to the little office where the interview was being held, and put the statement on the table. By it was a sheet of paper, on which he had scribbled a number of figures.

"This statement is entirely inaccurate," he said. "It seems to be dated three days ago, but it does not in any way represent Mr Lyne's account. It shows, for example, over two hundred thousand pounds on deposit account; the actual amount on deposit is less than fifty thousand – forty-eight thousand seven hundred, to be exact. Most of this has been transferred to the current account at some time or other, the actual cash remaining in that account being about five thousand pounds."

Surefoot whistled softly.

"Then you mean that the difference between the real condition of affairs and this statement is about two hundred thousand pounds?"

The accountant nodded.

"The moment I saw it I knew it was wrong. As a matter of fact, I paid a great deal of attention to this particular account, and I have twice suggested to the manager, Mr Moran, that he should write to Mr Lyne, pointing out the low state of his balance. As I say, we don't worry very much about moneylenders' balances, because very often they put all their available cash into loans."

"What about these stocks?"

"They're quite all right, with the exception of thirty thousand pounds' worth of Steel Preferred which were sold four months ago on Mr Lyne's instructions. The money received for that is in another account."

"Did you receive any letter from Lyne, in answer to yours?"

"In answer to the manager's?" corrected the accountant. "No, sir. I wouldn't see them anyway. They'd be on Mr Moran's file, where you'll probably find them."

Smith considered the matter.

"Did Mr Moran see Lyne last Tuesday, about ten o'clock in the morning?"

The accountant smiled.

"If he did, he didn't tell me. Last Tuesday morning?" He considered. "He didn't come in till about midday. He said he'd had an interview of some kind, but what it was I don't know." And then, very seriously: "There's something radically wrong, isn't there, and Mr Moran is in it? I will give you and the bank any help I can. As I said before, I know nothing whatever about these transactions. Would you like to see Mr Lyne's account? Very large sums have been going out in the past eighteen months, generally on bearer cheques. That is not unusual with a moneylender's account. It is customary to deposit promissory notes or acceptances against these withdrawals, but I understand that Mr Lyne has never done this."

He came back with a ledger, which Smith examined with an expert eye. Money had gone in sums of ten, fifteen, twenty thousand, and invariably through a Birmingham bank.

"Only one of these large cheques has been made payable to an individual," said the clerk, turning a leaf and pointing to a name. "It was whilst Mr Moran was on his holiday – "

Smith looked, and his jaw dropped. The name was Washington Wirth.

15

He stared at the entry for a long time.

"Can I get a trunk call through to this bank in Birmingham?" he asked.

Apparently there was some arrangement for facilitating inter-banking calls, for in a few minutes he was connected. The Birmingham bank manager confirmed all that he already knew. He did not know Mr Washington Wirth, though he had seen him once in his hotel. Apparently, when Mr Wirth opened his account, he was suffering from some complaint which confined him to bed and made it necessary that the blinds should be drawn. The manager's chief clerk who interviewed him had taken his signature, and that was the last that had been seen of him. He had an arrangement by which he could draw cash against cheques at three other branches of the bank, one at the London office, one at Bristol, and a third, which had never been used, at Sheffield. He invariably notified the Birmingham branch by telegraph that he was drawing money twenty-four hours before the cheque was presented; and although huge sums passed through his account, he had very little to his credit at that moment.

Surefoot Smith sent a detective to Birmingham with a number of specimen signatures, and instructions to bring back Wirth's.

Whoever was the giver of these midnight parties was certainly the man to whom large sums of money had been paid out of Hervey Lyne's account – possibly his murderer. He called up Dick, and, finding him working at his new model, told him as much as he thought was necessary of his discoveries.

"You're his next of kin and I suppose you ought to know this," he said.

Dick was staggered when he learned the amount of money that was missing.

"You haven't overlooked the possibility of Mr Wirth being Hervey Lyne himself, have you?"

"I've thought of that," said Surefoot. "The fact that he couldn't move without a bath-chair means nothing; that's one of the oldest fakes in the world. The cheques were undoubtedly signed by him. I've seen the last one; in fact, I've got it here."

He took it from his pocket. Turning it over, he saw what he had not noticed before – a scrawling pencil mark on the back. The mark was faint; it had evidently been written by one of those patent pencils which occasionally function and occasionally do not. Even so, an attempt had been made, which was partially successful, to rub off the inscription. With the aid of a magnifying glass the detective examined the writing and presently deciphered it.

"Don't send any more Chinese e…" Evidently the writing had wandered off the back of the cheque on to the blotting-paper where the old man wrote.

"Now what the devil does that mean?" asked Smith irritably. "There's no doubt about it being his writing. What does 'Chinese' mean? And who took the trouble to rub it off?"

He scratched his head in his exasperation.

"I ought to have asked the clerk if he'd got any Chinese bonds."

Dick lunched with Mary Lane and passed on to her all that the detective had told him. He was telling her about the cheque with the inscription on the back when he heard an exclamation, and looked at her in amazement. Her eyes and mouth were wide open; she was staring at him.

"Oh!" she said.

Dick smiled.

"Do you know anything about Chinese bonds?"

She shook her head.

"Tell me it all over again, and tell me slowly, because I'm not particularly clever."

He repeated the story about the faked account and the big cheques that had been drawn obviously to the credit of Mr Washington Wirth. Whenever she could not understand she pressed him for explanations, which he was not always able to give. When he had finished she sighed and leaned back in her chair. Her eyes were bright.

"You look terribly mysterious."

She nodded.

"I am mysterious."

"Do you think you know who killed that unfortunate old man?"

She nodded slowly.

"Yes; I wouldn't dare name him, but I really do think I have what the police call a clue. You see, I lived in Mr Lyne's house when I was a little girl, and there are some things I've never forgotten."

"I'll tell Surefoot – " he began.

"No, no." She was very insistent. "Dick, you mustn't. If you make me look foolish I'll never forgive you. My theory is probably utterly silly. I'll make a few enquiries before I even hint at it."

"In fact you're going to be a detective, darling," said Dick. "By the way, poor old Lyne's will has been discovered. I am his heir. The will is full of restrictions. For example, if I marry anybody outside my own nationality and religion I lose something, and if I reside out of England I lose something, and if I don't give his dog a good home I lose something more – his dog has been dead sixteen years, by the way – but, generally speaking, he's very generous and gives you about forty thousand pounds free of death duty – "

"Really!"

She was staggered at the old man's munificence; genuinely relieved, too, that in a moment of caprice he had not carried out the threat to disinherit his unpopular nephew.

Surefoot Smith did not know that the will had been found until he got back to his office, and, calling up Dick to congratulate him that afternoon, was annoyed to find that his news was old.

"As you're an interested party you'd better come down to the Yard right away. I've the bank accountant here and he's got something to say that will interest you."

Dick arrived to find the accountant looking rather bored in his shabby surroundings. Evidently the office arrangements at Scotland Yard did not impress him. He certainly shifted frequently in the hard seated kitchen chair which had been placed at his disposal. On Surefoot's table was a number of typewritten sheets of paper.

"This is the point," said Smith impressively, pushing the sheets for Dick to see them. "This gentleman, Mr – "

"Smith," said the accountant.

"That's very awkward," said Surefoot gravely. "Have you got any other name, such as Huxley or Montefiore?"

"Just Smith," smiled the accountant.

"Very awkward indeed," said Surefoot. "Most Smiths adopt another name. This is his name," he went on to explain. "Our friend here" (he studiously avoided calling his brother Smith by that name, and never afterwards did he employ it to describe the accountant) "says that the statement that was sent to Miss Lane was not typed at the bank or on any bank typewriter. He proved this conclusively from my point of view by giving me specimens from all the typewriters used at the bank. A very good bit of detective work, though I don't see that it carries us much farther forward, because, if, as we believe, Moran has been bilking these funds, he probably typed the statements at home. The blanks or forms are not difficult to get?"

The accountant shook his head.

"Oh no; they are printed by hundreds of thousands – "

"Could anybody outside the bank secure them?"

The accountant thought it was possible.

"It comes to this, then," said Surefoot, "that you're satisfied this statement was not typewritten in your bank?"

"Or by any bank machine," said the accountant. "Every branch office uses a" – he mentioned the name of an American make of machine – "and always the same type face is used, the same colour ribbon, the same carbons. The ribbon here is purple; we invariably use black. I didn't realise that till I made enquiries. The type face is entirely different."

He suggested the make of machine on which the statement had been written, and this afterwards proved to be correct.

Surefoot could not remember having seen a typewriter at Moran's flat. He accompanied Dick, after the accountant had gone, to Parkview Terrace, and made a more careful search. They found a portable typewriter, though it was unusable. Remembering the flat in Baynes Mews, Smith was not greatly depressed by his failure to discover the machine. It was possible, and even likely, that if Moran was the tenant of Baynes Mews, he would also have other places of call. In London there might be two or three flats engaged in false names (that in Baynes Mews had been engaged in the name of Whiteley), which Moran used for his own purpose – supposing it was Moran.

"Have you any doubts?" said Dick.

"I'm full of doubts," said Surefoot. "Some of 'em may be set at rest when I find Jerry Dornford. You remember, after we left Naylors Crescent and were going over to see the old man, Dornford passed in a car that was raising a noise like hell? And do you remember he slowed down just about opposite the place where the old man was sitting?"

"Well?" said Dick, when he paused.

"Well," said the other, indignant at his denseness, "didn't he have a gun of yours?"

"Good God! You don't think that Dornford killed him?"

"Why shouldn't he?" asked the other truculently. "He owed Lyne money, and Lyne had threatened to put him into the court unless he paid on the very day of his murder. If you know Dornford's reputation as well as I do, you know that that's the one thing he'd want to avoid. He prides himself upon being a swell, though his father was a horse dealer and his mother – well, I won't talk about her! Bankruptcy means being kicked out of all his clubs. A bird like that would do almost anything to avoid social extinction – is that the right word? Thank you very much."

"Where is he?"

"That's what I'd like to know," said Surefoot grimly. "He hasn't been seen since we saw him!"

16

Mr Surefoot Smith was one of those individuals who never seem to do any work. He was to be seen at odd hours of the day, and sometimes in odd places of the West End. It seemed that he was able to dispense with sleep, for you were as likely to meet him at four o'clock in the morning as at four o'clock in the afternoon.

He had a villa at Streatham.

"He is the type of man," Dick Allenby once described him, "who was foreordained to live with a married sister."

In addition, he had a room in Panton Street, Haymarket, and not the more fashionable part of Panton Street either. In all probability this was his real home, though the Streatham villa was not such a myth as his colleagues chose to imagine it.

Thieves knew him and respected him; the aristocrats of the underworld, who were his special prey, avoided him with great care, but not always with conspicuous success. He was the terror of the little card-sharping gangs; confidence men hated him, for he had put more of their kind in prison than any two officers of Scotland Yard. He had hanged three men, and bitterly regretted that a fourth had escaped the gallows through the lunacy of a sentimental jury.

His pleasures were few. Beer was more of a necessity than a dissipation; for how can one sneer at a man who consumes large quantities of malted liquor necessary for his well-being and happiness, and find anything commendable in the physical wreck who seeks, through copious potions of Vichy water, to combat the excesses of his youth?

In the privacy of his Panton Street room, he worked out his problems in a way peculiar to himself. He invariably wrote on white blotting-paper with a pencil, and seldom employed any other medium except when he was called upon to furnish a conventional report to his superiors. He invariably covered both sides of his blotting-paper with writing which nobody but he could read. It was a shorthand invented thirty years ago by a freakish schoolmaster, and the only man who had ever learned it thoroughly was Surefoot Smith. He had not only learned it, but improved upon it. It was his boast that no human being could decode anything he ever wrote; many had had the opportunity and tried, for after Mr Smith had finished with his blotting-paper it was passed on to junior officers for a more proper use.

He worked out Leo Moran's movements chronologically so far as they could be traced. One portion of the day previous to the murder had been clearly marked. Moran had broadcast a lecture on banking and economics. Surefoot Smith smiled at a whimsical thought. He would not die without honour, if he was the detective who brought about the execution of the first broadcaster.

After his lecture he had gone to the Sheridan Theatre; thence to Dick Allenby's flat. After that, home, where he had found a letter – Surefoot Smith conceded him the truth of this – which sent him in search of Mary Lane.

What had he been doing on the morning of the murder? Possibly the accountant had called him up and told him that his leave was not granted. Mr Accountant Smith had not said as much, but then between bank employees there was a certain freemasonry, and one didn't expect, or was a fool if one did, that they would tell everything about their comrades, even if they were comrades suspected of forgery and murder.

Surefoot Smith allowed also the element of self preservation to enter into the accountant's evidence. He himself might not be free from blame; the success of the forgery might be due in not a little measure to his own negligence. Everybody had something to hide – and possibly the accountant was no exception.

One thing was certain; the aeroplane had been ordered at a moment's notice. That was not the method by which Moran intended leaving the country.

What was the stock to the transfer of which he had been so anxious to get Mary Lane's signature? Without a very long and careful search it was unlikely that that question would be answered.

Jerry Dornford's disappearance presented a problem of its own. His manservant in Half Moon Street said he was not worrying; Mr Dornford often went away for days together, but where, the man could not say, because Mr Dornford was not apparently of a confiding nature. If the servant guessed, he guessed uncharitably. Here was a man also without money, and almost without friends. He had one or two who had country houses, but enquiries of these had produced no result. The servant remembered the names and addresses of a lady or two, but these could throw no light upon the mystery.

Dornford owned an estate in Berkshire. Part of it was farm land, which produced enough income to pay the interest on the mortgage; and if the mortgagees did not foreclose it was because a sale would bring only a portion of the money which had been advanced. There had been a house on the property, but this had been sold to a local golf club many years before, and all that remained of Gerald Dornford's possessions were about three hundred acres of pine and heather.

Here was a man who certainly could not afford two or three addresses.

The bullet had not been found, though the turf had been taken up, to the distress of the park authorities, and the ground sifted to the depth of a foot. There was a possibility that it might have passed at such an angle that it fell into the canal or against the opposite bank. It all depended on what angle the shot had been fired. If Surefoot Smith's first theory held ground and the old man had been killed by a bullet fired from a rifle on the upper floor of Parkview Terrace, the bullet should have been found within a few feet of where the chair had stood. If it had been fired from Dornford's car, it could hardly have passed through his body and reached the canal.

He was in constant touch with Binny, but the chairman could give no further information. He had not heard the whiz of the bullet as it passed him, not even heard its impact, and offered here a perfectly reasonable excuse, that the noise of Dornford's car would, had it coincided with the shot, have deadened all other sound.

It was four o'clock on a Saturday afternoon, and Surefoot Smith, who had spent most of the night on his feet, found himself dozing in his chair, a practice which for some reason he regarded as evidence of approaching senility. He got up, washed his face in the bathroom wash-basin, and went out into the Haymarket, not very certain as to the way he should take or in what direction he should continue his investigations.

He crossed Piccadilly Circus and was standing aimlessly watching a traffic block at the corner of Shaftesbury Avenue, when somebody bumped into him. His unconscious assailant was moving on with a muttered apology when Surefoot crooked his finger in his overcoat.

"What's the matter with you, Mike?"

There was reason for his surprise.

In twenty-four hours the appearance of Mike Hennessey had changed. The big face had grown flabby; heavy pouches were under his eyes; his unshaven face was a sickly yellow. Was it Surefoot's fancy, or did he turn a shade whiter at the sight of him?"

"Hullo!" he stammered. "Well…now…isn't that curious, meeting you?"

"What's the matter, Mike?" asked Surefoot.

It was his habit to suspect criminal intentions in the most innocent of men, and his very question was accusative.

"Eh? Nothing. I'm sort of walking about in a dream today…that play coming off and everything."

"I've been phoning you all the morning. Where have you been?"

Mike started.

"Phoning me, Mr Smith – Surefoot, old boy? I have been out of town. What did you want me for?"

"You weren't at your lodgings, you weren't at the theatre. Why were you keeping out of the way?"

Mike tried to speak, swallowed something, then, huskily: "Let's go and have a drink somewhere. I've got a lot on my mind, Surefoot, a terrible lot."

There was a brasserie in a side street near the Circus, where beer could not be legally supplied until six o'clock. Nevertheless they made for this spot and the head waiter bustled up with a smile.

"Do you want to have a little private talk, Mr Smith? You don't need to sit out here; the place is like a morgue. Come into the manager's office."

The manager's office was not a manager's office at all, except by courtesy. It was a very small private room.

"I'll bring you some tea, Mr Smith. You'll have coffee, won't you, Mr Hennessey?"

Hennessey, sitting with his eyes shut, nodded.

"What is on your mind?" asked Smith bluntly. "Washington Wirth?"

The closed eyes opened and stared at him. "Eh? Yes." He blinked at his questioner. "I think…well, he won't be in the theatrical business any more, and naturally that's worrying me, because he's been a good friend of mine."

He seemed to find a difficulty, not only in speaking, but in breathing. His chest puffed up and down, and then: "Is that what you wanted to see me about?" he asked jerkily.

"That was just what I wanted to see you about. He was a friend of yours?"

"A patron," said Mr Hennessey quickly. "I looked after him when he was in town. I didn't know very much about him except that he had a lot of stuff – money, I mean."

"And you didn't ask him where he got it, Mike?"

"Naturally," said Hennessey, avoiding his eyes.

The head waiter came at that moment with a tray which contained two large bottles of beer, a bottle of gin, cracked ice, and a siphon.

"Tea," he said formally, put it down, and left them.

Surefoot Smith was in no sense depressed as he broke the law.

"Now come across, Mike," he said, not unkindly. "I want to hear just who is this fellow Wirth."

Mike licked his dry lips.

"I'd like to know where I am first," he said, doggedly. "Not that I could tell you anything, Surefoot – not anything for certain. What's my position? Suppose I thought he was somebody else, and said: 'Listen – you either help me, or I'm going to ask questions.' "

"Yes, suppose you blackmailed him?" interrupted Smith brutally.

Mike winced at this.

"It wasn't blackmail. I wasn't sure – do you get my meaning? I was putting up a bluff. I wanted to see how far he'd go." And then suddenly he broke down and covered his face with his big, diamond-ringed hands, and began to sob. "Oh, my God! It's awful!" he moaned.

Other men would have been embarrassed; Surefoot Smith was merely interested. He laid his hand on the other's arm.

"Are you in on the murder? That's the question?"

Mike's hands dropped with a crash on to the marble-topped table. His ludicrous, tear-stained face was a picture of bewilderment.

"Murder?… What do you mean – murder?" He almost squeaked the question.

"The murder of Hervey Lyne. Didn't you know?"

The man did not answer; he was petrified with terror.

"Lyne…murdered!" He croaked the words. It was amazing to believe that he was the one man in London who did not know that a mysterious murder had been committed in Regent's Park on the previous day, because the newspapers were full of it. Yet Surefoot felt that this was a fact.

"Murdered…old Lyne murdered? My God! You don't mean that?"

"Of course I mean it. What do you think – that I'm trying to make you laugh?"

Mike Hennessey was silent; speech was frozen in him. He could only sit regarding the detective with round eyes from which all expression had died. Mike had a weakness for weeping, but he also had an unsuspected strength of will. When he spoke at last his voice was completely under control.

"That's shocking. I didn't read the newspapers this morning."

"It was in last night's," said Surefoot.

The other shook his head.

"I haven't read a newspaper since Thursday morning," he said. "Old Lyne! He was Miss Lane's guardian, wasn't he?"

He was fighting for time – time to get the last weakness in him crushed, and to build himself the reserve that would prevent his collapse.

"No, I've read nothing about it. It's curious how you miss things in newspapers, isn't it? I've been so worried over this theatrical business that I've practically taken no interest in anything else in the world."

"What work did you do for Wirth?"

Surefoot's voice was cold. He had dropped his boy-friend manner, was even without interest in the unopened bottle of beer.

"Did you draw money from the bank on his behalf?"

Mike nodded.

"Yes, I've done that for him – big sums of money. Gone to his bank and met him afterwards by appointment."

"Where?" sharply.

"At various places – railway stations; the Kellner Hotel mostly. He generally drew a big sum when he had his parties, and I used to hand it over to him before the guests came. He said he was a merchant in the Midlands, but to tell you the truth, Surefoot, I've always had my doubts about that. Still, he didn't look a crook, and some of the queerest mugs are rolling in money. Why shouldn't he have been? He's not the first jay that put up money for a theatrical production, and not the last, please God!"

"Which bank did you draw it from?"

Mike told him. It corresponded with the information which Surefoot already had.

"He generally gave me a letter to take to the bank manager, asking him to cash the cheque. I've been to Birmingham and Bristol and – "

"That's all right." Smith leaned heavily on the table. "Who was he – Washington Wirth?"

Mike shook his head.

"Honestly I don't know. If I die this minute I don't know. I got in touch with him after my last bankruptcy proceedings had appeared in the newspapers. He wrote to me and said how sorry he was that a clever man like me had got into trouble, and offered to finance me."

"A written note?"

"Typewritten. I've got the letter in my diggings somewhere. He asked me to meet him at the Kellner. That was before the parties started, when he had a smaller suite. I went. The only thing I knew about him was that he wore a wig and that he wasn't what he appeared to be; but I've never pried into his business – "

"That's a lie," said Surefoot. "You just told me that you blackmailed him."

"I didn't really. I put a bluff up on him. I knew he wasn't what he pretended to be; I had to guess what he really was."

He was lying: of that Surefoot Smith was perfectly certain.

"Does it occur to you that you're in rather a tight place if this man is ever arrested? I have reason to believe that he has misappropriated money, the property of the late Hervey Lyne, and I have also reason to believe that he killed the old man – and that's murder. You don't want to be mixed up in murder, Mike, do you?"

Michael Hennessey's face was contorted with anguish. He was almost incoherent when he spoke.

"I'd help you if I could, Mr Smith – but how can I? I don't know the man – I swear I don't know the man!"

Smith peered into his face.

"Do you know anything about Moran?"

The big mouth dropped.

"The banker?" he stammered.

"Do you know anything about the faked balance sheet which was sent by accident to Miss Lane?"

For a second Surefoot thought the man was going to faint.

"No – nothing; I know Moran – I know Wirth too."

He stopped, was silent a little while. "Suppose I found him – Wirth – what's my position then?"

Surefoot stood up.

"Your position is just the same whether you find him or whether we find him," he said roughly. "You don't seem to know what you've let yourself in for, Mike Hennessey. Here's a man been murdered – two men have been murdered – probably by the same hand. Tickler was killed for knowing too much. It might be safer for you if I put you inside."

A smile dawned on Mike's face.

"Am I a child?" he asked. He had got back his old poise. "How did I get out of the gutter – by taking notice of threats? Don't worry about me, Surefoot."

"There's a lot more I've got to say to you," interrupted the detective, "but just wait here till I telephone."

A momentary look of alarm came to the man's face.

"Don't worry; I'm not going to pinch you. I shouldn't want any assistance to do that."

There was a telephone booth in the outer room, and he called Scotland Yard urgently.

"Chief Inspector Smith speaking. I want two of the best men on duty to pick me up at Bellini's. I'm with Mike Hennessey, the theatrical man. He's to be under observation day and night from now onwards, and no mistakes must be made. Do you hear?"

They heard and obeyed. A quarter of an hour later, when they strolled out through the narrow side street to Piccadilly Circus, two young men followed them, and when Mike called a cab and drove off, a second cab carried the watchers.

Mike Hennessey was not at the theatre when the curtain rang down finally on *Cliffs of Fate*, and although the termination of this drama meant a search for new work, there was not one of the cast who did not breathe a sigh of relief when the muffled strains of the National Anthem came through the thick curtains.

Dick was reading the evening newspaper when Mary came into the dressing-room. The story of the Lyne murder was splashed over the front page; it included an interview with Binny and a talk with the park-keeper.

"I knew Mr Lyne very well by sight," said Jame's Hawkins, who had been a park-keeper for twenty-three years. "He always came into the gardens in the afternoon, and generally had a little nap before he was taken home. I've spoken a word or two with him, but he was not a gentleman who encouraged conversation. Mostly his attendant, Mr Binny, used to sit and read to him. I saw Mr Binny reading that afternoon, and went up to him and said: 'What's the good of your wasting your breath? The guv'nor's asleep.' Little did I think that he was dead! This is the second murder that we've had in the park in thirty-five years..."

Dick put down the paper when the girl came in, and prepared to make himself scarce.

"Sit down. I'm not going to change yet; I'm tired."

"Well, have you found your man?" he asked flippantly.

She did not smile.

"I think so," she said.

"Have you read the account?"

"I've read it – every ghastly line of it."

"Well," he challenged her, "is it Binny or the park-keeper?" And then, realising that flippancy was in the circumstances a little callous, he apologised.

"I don't know how it is, but I can discuss this murder as though it were of somebody I'd never heard of. The poor old man loathed me, and I'm sure if he could only have made up his mind as to who else would have taken better care of his fortune than I, he would have left the money to him like a shot! By the way, Binny has a theory of his own. I had a talk with him today. He favours Jerry Dornford; mainly, I think, because he doesn't like Jerry."

"Has Mr Smith told you all the clues he has?" she asked.

She had evidently paid no attention to Binny's theory.

"No, I can't say that he has. He's rather stuffy when it comes to his own business."

"Do you think he would tell me?"

He looked at her in amazement.

"My dear Mary – " he began.

"Don't 'dear Mary' me, or I shall be very rude to you," she said. "Do you think he would?"

She was quite serious and he changed his tone.

"If he thought you could help him I'm sure he would," he said. "He has promised to call here tonight and tell me the latest developments. Would you like me to ask him?"

"I'll ask him myself," she said.

Surefoot arrived very late and very ruffled. He was entitled to his annoyance, for at half-past seven that night a penitent young detective had called him on the phone and had confessed failure.

"You missed him?" roared Smith. "Two of you? What's the matter with you?"

"I'm sorry, sir, but he must have known he was being tailed, and he dodged through the Piccadilly Tube. I'd just turned my head and he was gone – "

"Turned your what?" sneered Surefoot. "All right; scour London and pick him up. You know his address. He's got to be found."

He came to the Sheridan, full of bitterness about the new generation of detectives.

"They expect everything to be done for them. They rely on science instead of their eyesight," he fumed.

"Here's a detective for you."

Dick indicated the girl, and to his surprise Surefoot showed no sign of impatience.

"I should say she's got more sense in her little finger than those – gentlemen have in their big, useless bodies."

He looked at her thoughtfully.

"I'm going to ask you something, Mr Smith," she said. "Would you tell me all you know about this case? I think I may help you."

Again Dick Allenby was amazed that the big man made no jest of the offer. He looked at her owlishly, opened his big mouth, closed it again, rubbed his head (going through his repertory, noted Dick mentally).

"Why shouldn't you?" he said at last. "Do you want him to know?" He jerked his head towards Dick.

She hesitated.

"If you don't mind. If you do we'll turn him out."

She was dressed for the street by the time the detective had arrived, and suggested that they should go to her flat. They went up in the lift together. Her flat was the last in the corridor. She went ahead of them, and stood stock still, showing an alarmed face to the two men.

The door was wide open!

"Did your servant leave it open?" asked Smith.

Surefoot pointed to the lock; the marks of a powerful jemmy showed where the door had been forced. The lock itself was hanging on one screw.

He went ahead, switched on the lights, without result.

"It's been turned off at the fuse box. Where is it?"

She indicated the position, and after a little fumbling there was a click, and light showed along the short passage.

"He fastened the door after he got in, but couldn't fasten it when he left."

Smith picked up two small wooden wedges from the floor.

He went out again into the corridor, the end of which was formed by a half wood, half glass door leading to the fire escape. He tried this, and, as he expected, found it open. A flight of iron stairs led into the darkness below. He sent for the liftman, who could give no information at all. On a Saturday night most of the people who lived in the flats, he said, were in the country, where they spent their weekends, and there had been no strange visitors that he could remember.

Surefoot went ahead down the passage into the flat, saw a door wide open, and entered Mary's bedroom. It was a scene of indescribable confusion; every drawer of every bureau had been taken out and emptied on the bed and roughly sorted. They found the same in the dining room, where the little secretaire desk, which she had locked before she went out, had been broken and its contents piled on to the table.

Mary gazed with dismay upon the scene of destruction, but was agreeably surprised when she found that a small box which had been in her desk drawer, and which had been wrenched open, still contained the articles of jewellery she had left there. They were valued at something over two hundred pounds, she told the detective.

"Then what on earth did they come for?" she asked.

On further inspection Smith found that even the waste bin in the kitchen had been turned bottom upward and sorted over. One valuable clue he discovered: a small kitchen clock had evidently been knocked off the dresser and had stopped at eleven-fifteen.

"Less than an hour ago – phew!" Surefoot whistled softly. "In a devil of a hurry, too. Now tell me who knows this place – I mean, who has been here before? Forget all your girl friends, but tell me the men."

She could enumerate them very briefly.

"Mike Hennessey has been here, has he? Often? I've seen all the rooms, haven't I?"

"Except the bathroom," she said.

He opened the door of this well-appointed little apartment, switched on the light, and went in. The intruder had been here too; the wash-basin was half filled with discoloured water.

"Hullo! What's that?"

Smith's eyes narrowed.

Level with the wash-basin, and a little to the right of it, the enamelled walls of the bathroom bore a red smear. The detective touched it; it was still moist. He looked at the tessellated floor. There was nothing, but on the edge of the white bath the smear occurred again.

Behind the door was a clothes hook, and here also there was a trace of red.

"He came in here first," said Surefoot slowly. "He had to wash his hands, and, turning on the tap, his sleeve brushed the wall. There was blood on it; he didn't notice this. He took his coat off and threw it on the edge of the bath. Then he changed his mind and hung it up."

"Blood?"

Mary stared at the gruesome stain.

"Do you think he hurt himself getting in?"

"No, we should have seen it on the floor or in the passage. Besides, the glass door of the corridor wasn't broken – I wonder where he got it?"

Surefoot considered all the possibilities in the shortest space of time.

"It beats me," he said.

Surefoot Smith went into the kitchen to re-examine the clock. He was no believer in coincidences, had seen the stopped clock too often featured in works of fiction to believe implicitly the story it told. But his inspection removed all doubt; the clock had not stopped, but was still ticking; the jolt had merely thrown the pin connecting the hands from its gear, and no clever clue-maker could have done that.

Mary had followed him into the kitchen, and watched him silently whilst he was making the examination.

"Now will you tell me?" she said quietly.

Surefoot Smith gaped at her.

"About – ?"

"You said you would tell me what you have discovered about Mr Lyne's murder."

He perched himself on the edge of the kitchen table, and briefly told her all he knew.

To say that Dick Allenby was surprised was to put it mildly. He regarded every Scotland Yard detective as reticence personified. Surefoot Smith was notoriously "dumb," and here he was talking freely to the girl, and, if he showed any embarrassment at all, it was the presence of Dick himself which provoked the inhibition.

Mary Lane sat, her hands clasped in her lap, her brow knitted.

"Got anything?" asked Surefoot anxiously.

And then he must have caught a glimpse of the astonishment in Dick Allenby's face, for he scowled at him.

"You think I'm being foolish, Mr Allenby? Get the idea out of your mind; I never am. Every woman has just the kind of mind that every detective should have and hasn't. No science in it – not that I mean to be disrespectful, Miss Lane – just plain common-sense. Got it?"

He addressed the girl again. She shook her head.

"Not quite," she said. "I know why they burgled my flat, of course."

Surefoot Smith nodded.

"But you can't quite understand how they came to think it was here?"

Dick interrupted.

"May I be very dense," he asked politely, "and enquire what this is all about? Didn't know what was here?"

"The bank statement," said Mary, without looking up, and again Smith nodded, a broad grin on his face.

"I guess that is what they came for, but I can't understand how they knew."

Surefoot chuckled.

"I am the clever fellow that gave it away," he said. "I told Mike Hennessey this afternoon that a bank statement had been sent to you. I didn't tell him that it was in my pocket, and I could have saved him a lot of time and trouble. It's a great pity."

He ran his hand irritably through his hair and slid off the table. "Those bloodstains now – they look bad," he said, and loafed out of the room with the other two behind him into the bathroom. "That's his sleeve – that's his hand, but too blurred to get a print. The man who came here wasn't hurt, and probably wasn't aware that he was bloodstained. Look at the top of that tap."

He pointed; there was a distinct smear of blood on the white-enamelled word "hot" on one of the taps.

Surefoot Smith took out his pocket torch and began to examine the passage-way. It gave him nothing in the shape of clues; but when he went outside the fireproof door, and inspected the door itself, he found two new traces of blood, one on the iron railings and one just below the glass panel of the door.

"I'll use your phone," he said, and a few minutes later was talking volubly to Scotland Yard.

Every railway station was to be watched; Dover, Harwich, Folkestone, and Southampton were to be warned.

"Not that he'll attempt to get out of the country. It's curious how seldom they do," he explained to the girl.

His offer to send up a man to be on guard outside the door she refused immediately, but he insisted, and in such a tone that she knew it would be a waste of time on her part to press her objection.

On his way home he called at old Lyne's house to interview Binny. That worthy man was in bed when he knocked, and showed considerable and quite understandable reluctance to open the door. No police had been left on the premises; Surefoot had been content to remove all documents to Scotland Yard for a closer scrutiny, and he sealed up the bedroom and the study.

Binny led him down to the kitchen, poked together the dying remnants of the small fire and dropped wood on it, for the night was a little chilly.

"I wondered who it was knocking – it brought me heart up into me mouth," he apologised, as he ushered the visitor into the tiny room. "I suppose, Mr Smith" – his voice was very anxious – "the old gentleman didn't leave me anything? I heard you'd found the will – mind you, I'm not going to be disappointed if he didn't. He wasn't the kind of man who worried very much about servants; he used to say he hated having them about the place. Still, you never know – "

"I haven't read the will thoroughly," said Surefoot, "but I don't seem to remember finding your name very prominently displayed."

Binny sighed.

"It's been the dream of my life that somebody would die and leave me a million," he said pathetically. "I was a good servant to him – cooked his food, made his bed, did everything for him."

The detective pushed over a carton of cheap cigarettes, and, still sighing, Binny selected one and lit it.

"There's one way you can help me, I think," said Smith. "Do you remember Mr Moran coming here?"

Binny nodded.

"Do you know what he came about?"

The servant hesitated a moment.

"I don't know, sir. But I have an idea it had something to do with his balance. Mr Lyne was a very curious old gentleman; he never wanted to see anybody, and when he did he was always a bit unpleasant to 'em."

"Was he unpleasant to Mr Moran?"

Binny hesitated.

"Well, I don't want to tell tales out of school, Mr Smith, but from what I heard he did snap a bit at him."

"You listened, eh?"

Binny smiled and shook his head.

"You didn't have to listen, sir." He pointed to the ceiling. "The study's above here. You can't hear what people are saying, but if a gentleman raises his voice as Mr Lyne did, you can hear him."

"You know Moran?"

Binny nodded.

"Do you know him very well?"

"Very well, sir. I was servant – "

"I remember, yes."

Surefoot Smith bit his lower lip thoughtfully. "Did he speak to you after his interview with the old man?"

Again Binny hesitated.

"I don't want to get anybody into trouble – "

"The trouble with you, Binny, is that you can't say 'yes' or 'no.' Did you see him?"

"Yes, sir, I did." Binny was evidently nettled. "I was taking in a letter that had come by post as he went out. And now, Mr Smith, I'll tell you the truth. He said a queer thing to me – he asked me not to mention the fact that he'd been, and slipped me a quid. Now I've told you all I know. I thought it was funny – but, bless your heart, he wasn't the first man to ask me not to mention the fact that they'd called on Mr Lyne."

"I suppose not."

On a little table near the wall was a small paper parcel, loosely wrapped. Surefoot Smith was blessed with a keen sense of smell; he could disentangle the most conflicting and elusive odours. But putty was not one of them; it had a pungent, and, to Surefoot Smith, an unpleasant aroma. He pointed to the parcel.

"Putty?"

Binny looked at him in surprise.

"Yes, sir."

"Have you been mending windows?" Surefoot looked up.

"No, sir, that was done by a glazier. I broke the scullery window this morning. I didn't like to call anybody in, so I did it myself."

"The trouble in this house is that you're always having windows broken," said Surefoot Smith. "Why didn't you report to the police the attempt to break into this house? Oh, I remember, Mr Lyne didn't want it."

When he went outside he made a more careful examination of the premises in the darkness than he had ever done by daylight. He went to the trouble of going to the back of the house, along the narrow mews, and here he saw how easy it was for a burglar to obtain admission. The back of the house was not protected, as most of its fellows were, by a garage block, and the door and window were approachable for anybody who could either scale the wall or force the door into the back courtyard. Was it a coincidence that this attempt had been made to gain admission into Lyne's house on the night of –?

Surefoot Smith frowned. It must have been the night that Tickler was murdered. Was there any connection between the two events?

He went back to Scotland Yard to receive reports, and found that his enquiries had produced no result. Berlin could tell him no more about Leo Moran, and there was absolutely no news at all of Gerald Dornford.

He opened the safe in a corner of his little room, took out the glove and the silver key, and laid them on the table. That key puzzled him. Was there any special reason why its owner should have gone to the trouble of painting it so elaborately and yet so carelessly? Any plater would have made a better job of it.

The glove told him nothing. He took from the big drawer of his desk a large sheet of virgin blotting paper and began to work out again the sum of his problem.

Tickler had been killed; old Lyne had been killed, possibly by the same hand, though there was nothing to connect the two murders. Leo Moran was, to all intents and purposes, a fugitive from justice, a man against whom could be made out a prima facie charge of felony. His disappearance had coincided, not only with the death of Lyne, but with the discovery that Lyne's bank account had been heavily milked.

Was he in Berlin at all? Somebody was very much interested in the recovery of the bank statement, had gone to the trouble of burgling Mary Lane's flat to recover it – who? One man at any rate knew, or thought he knew, that the statement was at Mary's flat, and that man was Michael Hennessey.

Mike's conduct that afternoon had been consistent with guilty knowledge. He knew, at any rate, who was Washington Wirth. The gentleman called Washington Wirth was a murderer, possibly a murderer twice over.

In disjointed sentences Surefoot wrote down his conclusions as they were reached; crossed out one and substituted another; elaborated some simple proposition in his mysterious shorthand, only to cross through the wriggly lines and begin all over again. He made a little circle that represented Mary, another for Dick Allenby, another for Gerald Dornford, a fourth for Leo Moran. At the bottom of the page he put a fifth circle for Lyne. How were they connected? What was the association between the four top circles and the fifth?

Between them he placed a larger O that stood for Michael Hennessey. Michael touched Washington Wirth, he touched Mary Lane, and possibly Moran. He crossed out this last conclusion and started again.

Gerald Dornford touched Dick Allenby; he could draw a straight line from Dick Allenby to the murdered man – a line that missed all and any intermediary.

He got tired after a while, threw down the pencil, and sat back with a groan. He was reaching for the key when the light went out. There was nothing very startling and nothing very unexpected about that: the bulb had been burning yellow for two or three days, and obviously required replacement. Surefoot Smith, in his lordly way, had demanded a fresh globe, and the storekeeper, in his more lordly way, had ignored the request. Without warning, the bulb had ceased to function.

Surefoot was rising to his feet to reach for the bell when something he saw stopped him dead. In the darkness the key was glowing like green fire. He saw the handle and every ward of it. And now he understood why it had such an odd colour – it had been treated with luminous paint.

He picked it up and turned it over. The under side was dull and hardly showed, for it had not absorbed the rays of the lamp.

Surefoot went out into the corridor and summoned an officer, and a little later a bulb was discovered and fixed. He examined the key now with greater interest, jotting down notes upon his already over-crowded blotting sheet.

He was beginning to see daylight, but only dimly. Then the telephone bell buzzed; he took it up, and, going to the officer on duty at the door, called him.

"If you see Mr Allenby, send him up."

He looked at his watch; it was twenty minutes past twelve, and he could only wonder what had brought Dick to Scotland Yard at such an hour. Possibly his gun had been recovered.

"I wondered if you were here," said Dick, as he came into the office and closed the door behind him. "I should have telephoned, but I was scared they wouldn't put me through to you."

"What's the trouble?" asked Surefoot curiously.

Dick smiled.

118

"There isn't any real trouble; only I've been – or rather, Mary has been – called up by Hennessey's housekeeper for information about the gentleman."

"Hasn't he come home?" asked Smith quickly.

"He wasn't expected home," said Dick. "The lady called up from Waterloo Station; she's been there since nine with a couple of Mike's trunks. He was leaving for the Continent by the Havre train, and had arranged for her to be there to meet him with his baggage. She waited till nearly twelve, got worried, and apparently called up several people who knew Michael, amongst them Mary. Fortunately, I was just leaving the flat when the woman telephoned."

"Have you been to his house?"

Dick shook his head.

"It wasn't necessary," he said. "He had a furnished flat in Doughty Street; he paid his rent and closed up the place tonight. Obviously he was making a getaway in rather a hurry. He didn't start packing till this afternoon."

"After he'd seen me," said Surefoot. He scratched his chin. "That's queer. I can quite understand his wanting to get away – as a matter of fact, he wouldn't have got any farther than Southampton; I had already notified the ports."

"You would have arrested him?" asked Dick, in amazement.

"There's no question of arrest, my friend," said Surefoot wearily. "It isn't necessary to arrest everybody you want to stop going out of England. Their passports can be out of order, the visa can be on the wrong page, the stamp can be upside down – there are a dozen ways of keeping the money in the country."

"Did Hennessey know this?"

Surefoot did not answer immediately.

"I can't understand it," he said slowly. "Of course he didn't know. That wouldn't have prevented him catching the train."

There was a knock at the door, and a pleasant looking man, whom Dick recognised as a chief inspector, came in.

"The Buckinghamshire police have got a case after your own heart, Surefoot," he said. "A regular American gang murder."

Surefoot became instantly alert.

"A gang murder, eh? What kind?"

"They call 'em ride murders, don't they? Somebody has taken this poor devil for a ride, shot him at close quarters, and thrown him out on to the sidewalk."

"Where was this?"

"On the Colnbrook bypass, this side of Slough. A big car passed, picked up the man lying across the footpath with its lights, and reported to the police. He couldn't have been dead more than half an hour when the police got to him."

"What is his description?" asked Surefoot.

"A big made man of forty-five," said the other, "wearing a green tie – "

"That was the tie that Mike Hennessey was wearing this afternoon!"

17

Mike Hennessey looked very calm, almost majestic in death; most easily recognisable. Surefoot Smith came out of the sinister little building and waited while the police sergeant turned the key.

Dick was waiting at the station. He had had enough of horrors for one night, and had not attempted to join himself in the identification.

"It's Mike all right," said Surefoot. "The murder was committed at ten-seventeen – there or thereabouts. The time is fixed by the big car that found the body, and a motor-cyclist who lives in this village reported to the police that he saw a small saloon car standing by the side of the road near where the body was found. I make out the two times as being between ten-fifteen and ten-twenty, and, allowing for the fact that the big machine did not overtake any car on the Colnbrook bypass, that puts the time at ten-seventeen. The murderer's car might have turned round and gone back. It could, of course, have gone right through the village of Colnbrook, avoiding the bypass, and I should imagine that is what happened. And now, my friend," he said seriously, "you realise that this was the gentleman who called at your young lady's flat? His coat must have been covered with blood without his realising the fact until, in searching the bathroom, he touched the wall with his sleeve. He took off his coat, washed his hands, and that's that."

"But surely some garage keeper will be able to identify the car if there was so much blood lost? The interior must be like a shambles."

Surefoot nodded.

"Oh yes, we'll find the car all right. There were three stolen last night that answer the description. I've just been through to the Yard and found that a machine has been discovered abandoned in Sussex Gardens."

A swift police car took them back to Paddington, and Surefoot Smith's surmise was confirmed. The abandoned car was that which the murderer had used. There was grisly evidence enough that the man had met his death in its dark interior – of other evidence there was none.

"We'll test the wheel for fingerprints, but Mr Wirth will have worn gloves."

"That lets out Moran, doesn't it?" said Dick.

Surefoot smiled.

"Where is Moran? In Germany, we say – he's as likely to be in London. You may get to Germany in a few hours and get back in a shorter time. It may not have been Moran who left at all."

"But why?"

Dick Allenby was bewildered, more than a little alarmed for Mary Lane's safety, and said as much. To his consternation, Surefoot agreed.

"I don't think she should stay in that flat. She may have other evidence, and now she's begun to theorise she might be dangerous to our friend."

He accompanied Smith to the police station whither the car had been taken, and found the usual scene of impersonal activity. There were photographers, fingerprint experts, car mechanics examining the speedometer. The owner of the car, who had been found and brought to the station, was a methodical man: he knew exactly the amount of mileage that was on the dial before the car was stolen, and his information helped considerably.

It seemed to Dick Allenby that he had spent the past fortnight examining bloodstained cars in police yards. There was a touch of the familiar in the scene he witnessed: the staring electric globes at the ends of lengths of flex, the peering police detectives searching every inch of the interior.

There was blood on the seat and on the floor; a trace of it on the gear lever. One of the detectives pulled a cushion from the driver's seat…

"Hullo!" he said, and, looking over his shoulder, Dick saw a flat silver cigarette case that was passed to Surefoot's hand.

Smith opened the case. It was empty. There was an inscription on the inside, easy enough to read in the light of the bulb.

"To Mr Leo Moran, from his colleagues in the Willesden branch, May, 1920."

Surefoot turned it over and over in his hand. It was an old case; there were one or two dents in it, but it was polished bright, and either was frequently used or had been recently cleaned. Surefoot held it gingerly by the help of a sheet of paper, and had it carefully wrapped. "We might get a fingerprint on that, but I don't think it's likely," he said. "It's a little odd, isn't it – being under the cushion?"

"He might have put it there and forgotten all about it."

Surefoot shook his head.

"It's not his car, it was pinched. As I say – it's odd."

He did not speak again for some time.

"I mentioned the fact that the young lady has the bank statement. Mr Hennessey passed the information on in the course of the ride, or before. The killer settled with Hennessey – by the way, he was supposed to be driving to Southampton to catch his boat. The car stopped at a filling station at the end of the Great West Road; Hennessey got out and telephoned to his flat – presumably to his housekeeper to send on his baggage. The murderer got rid of Hennessey as quickly as he could, rushed back to town and burgled the flat. Obviously he was somebody who had been there before – "

"Like Moran," suggested Dick.

Surefoot hesitated.

"He'll do as well as anybody else," he said. "He was looking for the bank statement. He couldn't have known that his coat was covered with blood, until he went into the bathroom, and saw either himself in the mirror or a stain on the wall. I'll tell you something more about him: he's lived in America. How's that for scientific deduction?"

"How on earth do you know that?"

"I don't," said the other calmly; "it's deduction – in other words, guesswork. It's a typical gang killing, though – taking a man for a ride and throwing him out of the car after he's been shot. Nobody seems to have heard the pistol go off, but if they did they'd think it was a motor-cyclist. They scorch down the bypass."

He drove home with Dick, and was very voluble. "Hennessey was in the swindle from the start. He knew who Wirth was, knew that Wirth was forging cheques, and took advantage of his knowledge to blackmail the other man." Then, abruptly: "I'm going to show Miss Lane the key and the cheque."

It was the first time Dick had heard about the key.

By the time Surefoot Smith reached Scotland Yard, all the grisly relics of the murdered man had been collected and laid on his table. There were a notebook, a few odd scraps of paper, about twenty pounds in cash, a watch and chain, and a keyring, but nothing that was particularly illuminating – except the absence of any large sum of money. Obviously, Hennessey did not intend to make his jump for the Continent on a capital of twenty pounds. Surefoot guessed that the murderer, profiting by the previous discovery of money in Tickler's pocket, had relieved him of what might have been very incriminating evidence.

He looked over the papers. One was a page torn from a Bradshaw, with pencil markings against certain trains. Surefoot guessed that Hennessey's plan was to make his way to Vienna.

The second paper was the more interesting. It was a sheet torn from a notebook, and contained a number of figures. Surefoot had a remarkable memory, and he recognised at once that the figures represented those balances which had appeared in the statement. Evidently the paper had been handled many times.

Smith was puzzled. Why had Hennessey taken the trouble to jot these notes down in pencil and keep them? Obviously he knew of the bank statement, had possibly concocted it; but here he would have some other data than this scrap of paper. If the bank statement was an invention, as undoubtedly it was, there was no need to keep this note. Either the man would invent the figures on the spur of the moment, or else he had some book record of the defalcations and the amount that should have stood to old Lyne's account.

Early the next morning he telephoned to Mary Lane, who had spent an uneasy night. She was not even stimulated by the knowledge that there was a police officer in the corridor outside her flat, one at the foot of the fire escape, and another patrolling before the house.

"Come round by all means," she said, and was relieved to know that she was seeing him, for she wanted advice very badly.

The morning had brought no news to Surefoot. The enquiries he had made had drawn blank. A search of Mike Hennessey's flat gave him no clue that was of the least value. Of papers or documents there was none; an old bank book told him no more than that three years before Hennessey had been living from hand to mouth.

He was rather despondent when he came into Mary's flat.

"It almost looks as if science has got to be brought in," he said gloomily, as he produced a small packet from his pocket and laid it on the table. "Maybe you're it!"

He opened the wash-leather wrapper and disclosed the key. Then from his pocket-book he took out a cheque and laid it on the table. She examined the faint pencil marks carefully and nodded.

"That is Mr Lyne's handwriting," she said. "I think I told you that when I was a girl I lived in the same house; in fact, I kept house for him, in a very inefficient way. He was rather trying to live with."

"In what way?" asked Surefoot.

She hesitated.

"Well, in many ways – domestically, I mean. For example, he had the same tradespeople for over forty years, and never changed them, although he was always quarrelling with them or disputing the amount he owed them."

She looked at the key, turning it over and over in her hand.

"Would you think I was terribly vain if I told you I thought I could find the man who killed Mr Lyne?"

"I think you would be very silly if you tried to do it on your own," said Smith bluntly. "This fellow isn't one you can monkey about with."

She nodded.

"I realise that. Will you give me a week to make enquiries?"

"Don't you think you'd better tell me what your suspicions are?"

She shook her head.

"No; I am probably making a fool of myself, and I have a very natural desire to avoid that."

Smith pursed his thick lips.

"You can't keep these – " he began.

"I don't want them," she said quickly. "You mean the cheque and the key? Would it be asking you too much to give me a replica of the key? If I find the lock it fits I'll telephone you."

He looked at her in surprise.

"Do you think you can find the lock?"

She nodded. Surefoot Smith sighed.

"This is like doing things in books," he said, "and I hate the way they do things in books. It's romantical, and romantical things make me sick. But I'll do this for you, young lady."

Two days later she received a brand-new, shining key, and set forth on her investigations, never suspecting that, day and night, she was shadowed by one of three detectives, whose instructions from Surefoot Smith had been short and not especially encouraging.

"Keep this lady in your sight. If you let her out of your sight, your chance of ever being promoted is practically nil."

It was the third day after the murder of Mike Hennessey that Cassari Oils moved. They had hovered between £1 3s. and £1 7s. for five years. They represented £40 shares, for in pre-war days they had been issued at 1,000 francs. The field was situated in Asia Minor, and had produced enough oil to prevent the company from collapsing, but insufficient to bring the shares back to their normal value.

Mary read the flaming headline on the City page, "Sensational Rise of Cassari Oils," and called up Mr Smith.

"Those were the shares that you transferred to Moran, weren't they?" he asked, interested. "What did they stand at last night? I haven't seen the paper."

The stock had jumped from 25s. to 95s. overnight. When Surefoot Smith put a call through to the City he was staggered to learn that they stood at £30 and were rising every minute.

He drove up to an office in Old Broad Street which supplied him with particulars of financial phenomena, and discovered the reason from an unconcerned stock-jobber.

"They struck big oil about three months ago, and they've been sinking new wells. Apparently they found inexhaustible supplies, but managed to keep it quiet until they'd cleared the market of every floating share. The stock is certain to go to a hundred, and I can advise you to have a little flutter. There's no doubt about the oil being there."

Surefoot Smith had never had a flutter in his life, except that he invariably had half a crown on some horse in the Derby which he picked with the aid of a pin and a list of probable runners.

"Who is behind this move?" he asked.

The jobber shook his head. "If I tried to pronounce their names I'd dislocate my jaw," he said. "They are mostly Turks – Effendi this and Pasha that. You'll find them in the Stock Exchange Year Book. They're a pretty solid crowd; millionaires, most of them. Oh no, there's nothing shady about them; they're as solid as the Bank of England, and this isn't a market rig. They haven't a London office; Jolman and Joyce are their agents."

To the office of Messrs. Jolman and Joyce Surefoot Smith went. He found the place besieged. He sent in his card and was admitted to the office of Mr Joyce, the senior partner.

"I can't tell you very much, Mr Smith, except what the newspapers can tell you. There are not a large number of shares on the market – I've just told a friend of mine who thought of running a bear that he's certain to burn his fingers. The only big holder I know is a man named Moran – Leo Moran."

18

Leo Moran! It was no news to Surefoot Smith that this man was interested in the stock, apart from the shares he had acquired from Mary. There was a little touch of trickiness about Moran; that was his reputation both in the bank and amongst his friends. From what Surefoot had gathered, and from his own knowledge of the man, he was capable of quixotic and generous actions, but, generally speaking, carried shrewdness a little beyond the line of fairness. Murderer he might be; forger, as Surefoot believed, he certainly was. The constant of his character was an immense self-interest. He was a bachelor, had no family attachments and few interests besides his shooting and the theatre.

This was a supreme gamble, then – Cassari Oils. Before Surefoot Smith left the stockbroker's office he discovered that Moran was, at any rate on paper, a millionaire. On one point he was puzzled: though Moran had bought steadily, and his operations had covered the years of defalcations, he had spent no very large sum, certainly only a small percentage of the moneys he was making. The man probably had other speculative interests, but these for the moment were impossible to trace.

Mr Smith went home to his rooms off the Haymarket, and was surprised to find a visitor waiting for him on the landing.

"I haven't been here two minutes," said Mary. "I got on to your secretary at Scotland Yard and he told me that you might be at your flat."

He unlocked the door and ushered her into his untidy sitting-room.

"Well, have you found anything?"

She shook her head and smiled ruefully.

"Only my limitations, I am afraid," she said, and sat down in the chair he pulled forward for her.

"You're giving it up, eh?"

She hesitated.

"No."

It required an effort of will to say "no," for she had awakened that morning with an intense sense of mental discomfort and a realisation of the difficulties which beset her. She had been half inclined to send a penitent note enclosing the key to Surefoot, but confidence – not much, but some – had come to her with breakfast, and she had decided upon this, what was to her, a bold move.

"I realise what I have undertaken," she confessed. "Being a detective is not an easy job, is it? Especially when you don't know things."

Surefoot smiled.

"The art of being a detective is to know nothing," he said oracularly. "What do you know? If you know anything less than I do, you haven't heard of the murder. On the other hand, it is possible you may know a great deal more."

"You are being sarcastic."

He shook his head.

"I don't know the word, Miss Lane. What is it you want to know?"

She consulted a little notebook she took from her pocket.

"Can you give me a list of all the big cheques that were cashed and the dates? I particularly want to know the dates. If my theory is correct, they are made out on the seventeenth of the month."

Surefoot sat back in his chair and stared at her. "That is a bit scientific," he said, a little resentfully, and she laughed.

"No, it is horribly like a mystery story. But, seriously, I do want to know."

He pulled the telephone towards him and called a number.

"Funnily enough, that is a bit of information I had never thought of getting," he said.

129

She felt he was a little nettled that he had been remiss in this respect, and she was secretly amused.

"But then, you see, Miss Lane," he went on, "if I had been at the Yard I would probably get it for you – hullo!"

He had got through to the bank. It took some time before the accountant, with whom he eventually got in touch, was able to supply him with the dates.

The cheques were made out on the 17th of April, the 17th of February, the 17th of December, the 17th of May in the previous year – Surefoot jotted down a dozen of them. Hanging up the receiver, he pushed the paper across to the girl.

"I thought so!" Her eyes were very bright. "Every one of them on the seventeenth!"

"Marvellous!" said Surefoot. "Now will you tell me what that means?"

She nodded.

"I will tell you in a week's time. I am going to do a lot of private investigation. There is one thing I wanted to speak about, Mr Smith." Her voice was troubled. "I don't know whether I am imagining things, but I have an idea that I am being very carefully watched. I am sure a man was following me yesterday. I lost sight of him in Oxford Street; I was looking in a shop window in Regent Street and saw him again. Rather an unpleasant-looking man with a fair moustache."

Surefoot Smith smiled.

"That is Detective Sergeant Mason. I don't think he is much of a good looker myself."

"A detective?" she gasped.

Surefoot nodded.

"Naturally, my dear young lady, I am taking great care of you. You might as well know that you are being shadowed, not because you are under suspicion, but because for the moment you are under our protection."

She heaved a sigh.

"You don't know how relieved I am. It was rather getting on my nerves. As a matter of fact, I don't think I should have come to see you at all but for this."

"What about the seventeenth?" asked Surefoot. "Don't you think it would be wise for you to tell me what your suspicions are about?"

She shook her head.

"I am being mysterious and rather weak," she said.

Her mystery certainly irritated Dick Allenby, who could never be sure of finding her at home. He had a talk with Surefoot and sought his help.

"She will be running into all sorts of danger," Dick complained. "This man obviously will stop at nothing. He may still think that she has got the bank statement."

"Have you seen the young lady at all?"

Surefoot opened another bottle of beer dexterously. He was sitting on a bench in Dick's workroom.

"Yes, I have seen her. She wants me to lend her Binny."

"Lend her Binny?" repeated the detective. "What does that mean?"

"Well, he is in my employ now. She says she wants enquiries made about a former servant of Mr Lyne's who is living in Newcastle under an assumed name. She wants Binny to go and identify the woman. I saw Binny about it, and he remembers her. She left soon after he arrived. She was a fairly old woman. Apparently she had a dissolute son who was a pretty bad character. Binny doesn't remember him, but Mary does. The old lady, who must be nearly ninety, is living in the north, and Mary wants him to go up to make sure that she hasn't made a mistake."

Surefoot Smith looked at him glumly.

"She told me nothing about it. Binny's your servant now? I suppose you own the house. What are you going to do with it?"

"Sell it," said Dick promptly. "In fact, I've already had an offer."

There was a knock at the door; the caretaker came in with a telegram for Dick. Surefoot saw him open it, watched him idly, and saw his jaw drop as he read it. Without a word be passed the wire across to Smith. It had been handed in at Sunningdale, and ran:

"Re patent air-gun reported stolen from you. Machine answering description circulated has been found at Toyne Copse lying at the bottom of a hole beneath body of a man believed to be G Dornford, of Half Moon Street. Please report immediately Sunningdale police station to identify property."

19

He and Surefoot went down into Berkshire together. He had no difficulty in recognising the rusted steel case which had once been a delicate piece of mechanism. He left it to Surefoot Smith to make other and more grisly identification.

Surefoot returned after visiting the place where the body had been found, and he had further and convincing information. Jerry Dornford's car had also been discovered less than a hundred yards from the place where he had died. The car had evidently been driven over the heath land and concealed in a small copse.

"It's Dornford's own property, and I don't think there will be much difficulty in reconstructing the accident which put him out," said Surefoot. "He had an evening newspaper in the car with him; it is dated the day of old man Lyne's murder."

"Poor devil! How was he killed – or was it a natural death?" asked Dick?"

Surefoot shook his head.

"An accident. The gun was loaded, wasn't it? Well, you'll be able to take the thing to pieces and tell me if it is still loaded. I should say it wasn't. Dornford stole the gun: there's no doubt about that. He either got scared or couldn't sell it, and decided to take it into the country and bury it. Very naturally, he chose a bit of land which is his own property. He took a spade with him – we found that. When they found him he was in his shirt sleeves. He had evidently dug the hole and was in the act of pushing in the gun when it went off. The bullet went through his body; we found it in a pine-tree that was immediately in the line of fire. In his pocket we found a demand for the payment of a loan, from Stelbey's, who did most of old Lyne's work. We also found a few notes that are going to make it pretty uncomfortable for somebody called Jules, when we can trace him."

"I can help you there," said Dick, who knew and rather disliked that sleek young man.

They came back to town late in the evening, and Surefoot was rather depressed.

"I always thought that Dornford had something to do with the murder, and put him down as a 'possible.' But it's pretty clear that he couldn't have done it, unless there were two bullets in the gun, or unless he understood the mechanism."

Dick went in search of Mary that night to tell her the news. He had never liked Gerald Dornford, but there were moments when he thought that his dislike was not so actively shared by the girl; but here he did her an injustice. A woman's instincts are keener than a man's, and she had placed Jerry in the definite category of men to be avoided.

She did not get back to her flat till late that night, as he discovered after repeated rings, and it was an unusually exhilarated voice that answered him when eventually he reached her.

"I've had a marvellous day, Dick, and I'm going to surprise our friend tomorrow – no, not tomorrow, the next day."

He tried to break the news gently about Jerry, and was surprised and a little annoyed to find his sensation was discounted.

"I read it in the evening newspaper. Poor man!" she said.

Dick Allenby spent a disturbed night. He was getting very worried about the girl and the risks she was taking. When he rang her in the morning she had already gone out, but when he saw Surefoot that gentleman did much to allay his anxiety.

"I've got the cleverest shadower at Scotland Yard following her night and day; you needn't worry." And then, curiously: "She hasn't told you what line she's following? The only thing I can find from my men is that she's chasing round the suburbs of London, and that she's doing a lot of shopping."

"Shopping?" repeated Dick incredulously. "What sort of shopping?"

"Pickles mostly," said Surefoot Smith, "though she's been after ham, and took over an hour in the City the other day buying tea. She's being scientific."

If the truth were told, Mr Smith found it increasingly difficult to avoid being very annoyed with his mysterious collaborator. He hated mysteries.

Mary had gone a little outside of her usual orbit of enquiry that day. She left early for Maidstone and spent the greater part of the morning talking with a country bootmaker, an ancient and a prosy gentleman with a poor memory and a defective system of book-keeping. She got back to town about five, feeling tired, but a hot bath and two hours' rest revivified her. She was bright and fresh when she buttoned up her long coat and went out.

It was ten o'clock; the sky was overcast and a sprinkle of rain was falling when she signalled a taxi and drove to King's Cross. She found the disconsolate Binny waiting on the platform. Although the night was warm he wore an overcoat and a muffler, and was a typical picture of misery and loneliness when she came up to him. The detective who had followed her watched them talking, and was slightly amused, for he had been told something about the object of this northward journey of Mr Lyne's handyman.

If he was amused, Binny was sceptical.

"I don't suppose I'll remember her, miss. People change, especially oldish people. She was only in the house about three weeks after I took on the job."

"But you would recognise her?" insisted the girl.

He hesitated.

"I suppose I would. I must say, miss," he protested, "I don't like these night journeys. I was in a railway accident once, and my nerves have never got over it. What with poor Mr Lyne's death and all the newspaper reporters coming to see me, I've got in such a state that I don't know whether I'm on my head or my heels."

She cut short his personal plaint with a repetition of her instructions.

"You will go to this house and ask to see Mrs Morris – that is the name she has taken, possibly because her son has been getting into trouble – "

"Visiting the sins of the parents upon the children I've heard about; visiting the sins of the children on the parents is something new."

"If it is Mrs Laxby you are to send me a wire, but you must be absolutely sure it *is* Mrs Laxby. You've got the photograph of her I gave you?"

He nodded miserably.

"I got it. But ain't this a job for the police, miss?"

"Now, Binny," she said severely, "you're to do as you're told. I've got you a nice sleeping car and it will be a very comfortable journey."

"They turn me out at four o'clock in the morning," said Binny; and then, as though he realised he was probably going a little too far with one who had such authority, he added, in a more cheerful tone: "All right, miss, you leave it to me; I'll send you a wire."

She left the platform a few minutes before the train pulled out, and took another taxi. The detective who followed her had no doubt that she was going back to her flat, and contented himself with giving instructions to his driver to follow the cab in front. Taxi-men are not necessarily good detectives, and it was not until the cab he was shadowing had set down an elderly man at a temperance hotel in Bloomsbury that he realised he was on the wrong trail, and doubled back to the flat to pick her up.

She had not returned, and, in a sweat, he began to cast round before reporting his failure to his very unpleasant superior.

It was a quarter past eleven when he saw the girl walking quickly in the opposite direction to which his cab was moving. He recognised Mary, jumped out of the cab, paid the driver, and followed through the rain on foot.

20

Unconscious of the fact that she had been shadowed, Mary Lane reached her objective. She was in a small paved courtyard which was made faintly malodorous by the presence of an ash-can that had not been emptied for a week. She moved cautiously, finding her way forward step by step with the aid of a tiny electric torch which she had taken from her handbag. At the end of the courtyard was a small door, flanked on one side by a window.

For a little while she stood on the doorstep, listening. Her heart was beating faster; she was curiously short of breath. Her early morning resolution to abandon her ridiculous quest came back with a stronger urge. It was absurd of her, and a little theatrical (she told herself) to continue these excursions into a realm in which she had no place. Police work was, in its most elementary phase, men's work.

The quietness of the night, the sense of complete isolation, the gloom and drabness which the falling rain seemed to emphasise, all these things worked on her nerves.

She took from her bag the replica key that Surefoot had had cut for her, and, finding the keyhole, pushed in the key. The truth or futility of her theory was to be put to the test.

For a moment, as she tried to turn the key, it seemed that she had made a mistake, and she was almost grateful. And then, as she slightly altered its position, she felt it turn and the lock snapped back with a loud "click!"

She was trembling; her knees seemed suddenly incapable of supporting the weight of her body; her breathing became painfully shallow. Here her experiment should have ended, and she should have gone back the way she came, but the spirit of adventure flickered up feebly and she pushed open the door. It opened without sound, and she peered into the dark interior fearfully. Should she go in? Reason said "No!" but reason might be womanly cowardice – a fear of the dark and the bogies that haunt the dark.

She pushed the door open wider and went in one step. She flashed the lamp around and saw nothing.

Then out of the darkness came a sound that froze her blood – the whimpering of a woman.

Her scalp tingled with terror; she thought she was going to faint. It came from below her feet, and yet from somewhere immediately before her, as though there were two distinct sounds.

The beam of light she cast ahead wobbled so that she could not see what it revealed. She steadied her arm against the wall and saw what looked like a cupboard door. To this she crept and listened.

Yes, the sound came from there and below. It was the entrance to a cellar. She tried the cupboard door; it was locked. And then there came to her an unaccountable fear, greater than any she had experienced before – there was danger, near, very near; a menace beyond her understanding.

She turned and stood, petrified with horror. The door was slowly closing. She leaped forward and caught its edge, but somebody was pressing it, and that somebody was in the room, had been standing behind the opened door all the time she had been there.

As she opened her lips to scream a big hand closed over her mouth, another gripped her shoulder and jerked her back violently, as the door closed with a crash.

"Oh, Miss Lane, how could you?"

The mincing tone, the falsetto voice, the artificial refinement of it were unmistakable. She had heard that voice at Kellner's Hotel when she had met Mr Washington Wirth. She struggled madly, but the man held her without difficulty.

"May I suggest, my dear young friend, that you keep quiet and save me from the necessity of cutting your darling little throat?"

Behind the spurious courtesy of that hateful voice lay a threat, horribly, significantly sincere. She knew him now: he would kill her with as little compunction as he would slaughter a rabbit. It was not perhaps expedient to carry out this threat immediately, and her only hope of salvation lay with her wits.

With a moan she went limp in his arms, and he was so unprepared for this that he nearly dropped her and dropped with her, for the sudden collapse almost threw him off his balance. Clumsily he laid her down on the stone floor.

She heard his exclamation of anger, and, after a while the jingle of keys. He was unlocking the cupboard door.

Noiselessly she rose and felt for the door knob. It turned without a sound, and in a second she had flung open the door and was racing across the courtyard. He was too late to stop her, and she was in the deserted side street before he recovered from his surprise. A few minutes later she had reached a main road; ahead of her she saw two policemen, and her first instinct was to fly to them and tell them of her adventure. She hesitated; they would think she was mad, and besides –

"Hullo, Miss Lane! You gave me a fright." It was the detective who had been following her all the evening, and he did not hide his relief. "Where on earth did you get to? I'm Stenford from Scotland Yard. Mr Smith told me that you knew I was trailing you."

She could have fallen on his neck in her gratitude – she was horrified to discover that she was hysterical. She gasped her story; he listened, incredulous.

"Have you got the key?"

She shook her head: she had left it in the door.

"I'll take you home, Miss Lane, and then I'll report to Mr Smith."

He was a young detective, full of zeal, and he had hardly left her at the door of her flat before he was racing back to conduct a little investigation on his own before reporting the sum of his discovery to Surefoot Smith.

Mary made herself a cup of tea and sat down to steady her nerves before she went to bed. The flat seemed terribly lonely. Odd noises, common to all houses, kept her jumping. She realised that she would not sleep that night except in other and less nerve-wearing surroundings, and was reaching for the telephone when its bell rang sharply – so unexpectedly that she jumped.

It was the voice of Surefoot Smith, urgent and anxious.

"That you, Miss Lane? Listen – and get this quickly! Go to your front door and bolt it! You're not to open the door until I come – I'll be with you in ten minutes."

"But – "

"Do as I tell you!"

She heard a click as he rang off. She was in a panic. Surefoot would not have been so alarming unless her situation was a perilous one.

She went out into the hall. It was in darkness. She knew that she had left a light burning. Acting on blind impulse, she darted back into the room she had left, slammed the door and shot home a bolt.

As she did so a heavy weight was flung against the door, the weight of a man's body. There were no arms in the room – nothing more formidable than a pair of scissors.

Crash!

The door shook; one of the panels bulged. She turned quickly and switched out the light.

"I have a revolver and I'll fire if you don't go away!" she cried.

There was a silence. She flung up the window. She must be a good actress or die.

"Mr Smith! Is that you? Come up the fire escape!" She screamed the words.

Again the door crashed, and she had an inspiration. She took up the telephone.

"Get the police station – tell them a man named Moran is trying to break into my room – Leo Moran – please remember the name in case anything happens…"

She left the receiver off and crept to the door. Stealthy feet were moving along the corridor; the sound became less audible and ceased.

Mary Lane sank down on to the floor, and this time there was nothing theatrical in her swoon. It was the frantic knocking on the door and the voice of Dick Allenby that brought her, reeling, to her feet. She drew the bolt to admit him and the detective. She had hardly begun to tell her story when she fainted again.

"Better get a nurse," said Surefoot. "Phew! I never expected to find her alive!"

An agitated Dick, engaged in bathing the white face of the girl, was not even interested to ask how Surefoot learned of the girl's danger. Mr Smith's officer had found him at his club and the two men had arrived simultaneously.

"I got a phone call from the detective who was shadowing her, giving me the story she had told. I told him to go straight back to her flat and stay there till I came. About half an hour later the simpleton called me up and said he'd searched the place and found nobody. Can you beat that? And then, of course, a trunk call from Birmingham came on the line and cut me off. I got rid of it and called Miss Lane – I should have called the nearest police station, but I worked it out that I'd be at the flat before they could deal with the matter. My officer called you at your club and got you?"

Mary had opened her eyes, and a few minutes later was sitting up, very white and shaken, but calm enough to tell her story. Throughout that night Scotland Yard officers combed London and the suburbs for their man. "May be accompanied by a woman," the official warning ran, and there was added a description of the wanted pair.

On the advice of Surefoot, Mary moved into an hotel. It was a quiet hostelry near the Haymarket. Surefoot had an idea that no harm would come to the girl now that Mr Washington Wirth's secret was out. He might kill her to avoid the embarrassment of identification, but now that she had spoken she was no longer a menace to his security.

"I hope so, at any rate," she said ruefully. "I am a failure as a detective."

Surefoot sniffed.

"I'm a bad man to ask for compliments," he said. "Beyond the fact that you've found our man and proved it, and apart from what I might call the circumstance that you've discovered how the forgeries were wangled, you've been perfectly useless!"

On the night of the girl's adventure Surefoot had cabled to his friend in New York the particulars of the English gangster who was at large in England. He went farther and arranged for the New York Police Department to cable the photograph of the man to Scotland Yard. A description would have been sufficient. There was no mistaking. The day the photograph was received, Surefoot had gone to call on the directors of Moran's bank. A very careful audit had been made of the bank accounts, but no further defalcations had been unearthed.

He was leaving when the general manager, who had placed the facts before him, remarked: "By the way, I suppose you know that Moran's service in the bank was interrupted when he went to America? He was there three or four years. We have reason to believe that he was engaged in some sort of speculative business – he never gave us any particulars about it."

"That's odd," said Surefoot.

He did not explain where the oddness lay.

"He has also a large interest in Cassari Oils, which have had such a sensational rise," said the manager. "I only discovered this a few days ago."

"I have known it for quite a long time," said Surefoot grimly, "and I can tell you something: he has made nearly a million out of the stock."

The man's eyebrows rose.

"So there was no need for him to be dishonest?"

"There never was," said Surefoot cryptically.

In these days Dick Allenby was a busy man. As principal heir to his uncle he had an immense amount of work to do. The late Mr Lyne had certain interests in France which had to be liquidated. Dick took the afternoon boat express to Paris.

Between Ashford and Dover there had been a derailment on the day before, and the passenger trains were being worked on a single line. There was very little delay occasioned by this method of working the traffic, except that it necessitated the boat train being brought to a standstill at a little station near Sandling Junction.

The Continental train drew slowly into the station and stopped. There was another train waiting to proceed in the opposite direction. As they were going to move Dick turned his head idly, as passengers will, and scrutinised the other passengers.

The Pullman car was passing at a snail's pace. The long body drew out of view and there came a coupé compartment at the end of the car. A man was sitting in the corner, reading a newspaper. As the trains passed he put the paper down and turned his head. It was Leo Moran!

21

Leo Moran!

It was impossible to do anything. The train was gathering speed and its next stop was Dover. Surefoot must be told. He might get through by telephone to London, but doubted if he had the time without missing the boat. Fortunately, when he arrived at Dover Harbour Station and came to the barrier where passports are examined, he recognised a Scotland Yard man who was scrutinising the departing passengers. To him be explained the urgency of the matter.

"He didn't come through this port," said the detective, shaking his head. "The train you saw was the one connecting with the Boulogne–Folkestone route. I'll get through to Mr Smith at once. I've had a very full description of Mr Moran for a long time, and so have the officers at Folkestone – I can't understand how they missed him."

Smith was not in his office when the call came through, but it was relayed to him almost immediately. Officers were sent to meet the train, but on its arrival there was no sign of Moran. Surefoot afterwards learned that it had been held up at South Bromley Station, and that a man who had occupied a coupé had alighted, given up his ticket, carrying his own baggage, which consisted of a small expanding suitcase, to a station taxi.

He had evidently acted on the impulse of the moment, according to the Pullman car attendant, for when, late that night, the taxi-driver was interviewed, it was learned that Moran had been driven to another station within a few miles of Bromley, and had gone on to London by the electric train.

A call at his flat produced no result. The porter had not seen him. Surefoot put a phone call through to Paris and spoke to Dick.

"You've got the keys of this man's flat, haven't you?"

"Good Lord! Yes, I'd forgotten them. They're in my workroom. See the housekeeper. You will find them…"

Smith was less anxious to find the keys than to establish the fact that Leo Moran had not returned. He would naturally call at Dick's place to retrieve the keys, and with this idea in his mind Smith put Dick Allenby's apartments under observation. But Moran did not come near. Either he knew that he was being sought and had reason for keeping out of the way, or he had some other establishment in London about which the police knew nothing.

The second enquiry which Surefoot Smith conducted was even more profitless. At the moment, however, he concentrated upon Moran. The register of every hotel in London was carefully scrutinised.

Mary Lane knew nothing about the discovery, and when Surefoot Smith saw her that evening be made no reference at all to the man Dick Allenby had seen. He made it a practice to call once or twice a day, for, although he was satisfied that there was no immediate danger to the girl, and that every reason for menacing her had disappeared now that the murderer of Hervey Lyne was identified, he took no chances. Men who killed as ruthlessly as "Mr Washington Wirth" were capable of deeper villainies.

Mary's hotel was an old-fashioned block set in the heart of the West End and in one of the most pleasant backwaters. Its furnishings were Victorian, its equipment a little primitive. As a reluctant concession to modern progress its ancient proprietor had installed gas fires in its bedrooms – it was the last hotel in London to adopt electricity for lighting.

The servants were old and slow; its proprietor still regarded the telephone as an unwarranted intrusion upon his privacy. There was one instrument, and that part of the office equipment.

It had its advantages, as Mary found. It was quiet; one could sleep at night. Strange guests rarely came; most of its patrons were part of the great shifting family that had made a habit of the hotel for years and years. Her room was pleasant and bright; it was on the street, and had the advantage of a narrow balcony which ran the full length of the building – a theoretical advantage perhaps, for nothing happened in that quiet street which made a balcony view desirable.

Mr Smith called the next evening, and was unlucky. If he had been a few minutes earlier he would have followed a sturdy figure that mounted the broad stairs and stood patiently whilst the hotel porter unlocked the next door to Mary's bedroom, before ushering Mr Leo Moran into the room he had engaged. He had not signed himself Leo Moran in the hotel register, but he had good and sufficient reason for that omission. He was plain Mr John Moore from Birmingham.

He ordered a light meal to be sent up to him, and when that had come and had been cleared away he locked the door of his room, opened a portfolio, and, taking out a number of documents and a writing pad, became immediately absorbed in the task he had set himself.

There was nothing flimsy about this hotel; the walls were thick; otherwise, he might have heard Surefoot Smith offering astounding theories concerning a certain fugitive from justice.

Surefoot's visit was not a very long one, and, following her practice, the girl read for an hour. Her nerves were calmer; she had got over the shock of that ghastly night. She had asked Surefoot to allow her to go back to the flat.

"I'll give you another week here," he said, shaking his head. "I may be wrong, but I have an idea I can liquidate this business in that time."

"But now that I've recognised him, and the police have circulated his name and description, there is no reason why he should do me any harm," she protested. "I am perfectly sure that it was not revenge, but self-preservation – "

"You can't be sure of anything where that bird is concerned," interrupted Smith. "You've got to allow for the fact that he's a little mad."

"Is he the man the American detective spoke about?" she asked curiously.

Surefoot Smith nodded.

"Yes, he's been in Chicago and New York for a few years, and was associated with some pretty bad gangs. The curious thing is that, even in those days, the stage had a fascination for him. He used to give hectic parties to theatrical people, and even appeared on the stage himself, though be wasn't a very great success. Out of his loot he financed a couple of road companies – it's the same man all right."

Mary was getting weary of the restrictions imposed on her; resented the early-to-bed rule which the doctor had prescribed. She lay in bed, very wakeful, heard ten and eleven strike, and was no nearer to sleep than she had been when she lay down.

Some time before midnight she fell into a doze, for she did not remember hearing twelve o'clock strike. She must have been lying, half asleep, half awake, for an hour, when something roused her to complete wakefulness. She shivered and pulled the clothes over her shoulders, and at that instant became wide awake.

The French window, which she had lightly fastened, was wide open; a draught of chill air swept through the room, the door of which was half open. She had locked it from the inside – she remembered that distinctly.

As she stood by the side of the bed a man's figure appeared in the doorway, silhouetted against the dim light in the passage outside. For a second she stood, petrified with fear and astonishment. Then she recognised that stocky figure, and the terror of death came to her, and she screamed.

The man stepped backwards and disappeared. She flew to the door, closed it with a crash, and turned the key. Switching on the light, she rang the bell urgently and repeatedly; closed and latched the French windows, and sat quaking, until she heard a knock at the door and the voice of the night porter, the one able-bodied servant of the hotel.

Slipping into a wrap, she opened the door to him and told him what had happened. His expression was one of profound incredulity.

147

He did not say as much, but she realised that he thought she had been dreaming.

"A man, miss? Nobody's passed me. I've been in the hall since ten."

"Is there no other way he could have got out?"

He thought a moment.

"He might have gone by the servants' stairs. I'll find out. Have you lost anything?"

She shook her head. "I don't know," she said impatiently. "Will you please call Superintendent Smith at Scotland Yard? Tell him I want to see him – that it's very, very important."

She went back to her room, locked the door, and did not come out again until Surefoot's reassuring voice accompanied his knock. She opened the door to him thankfully, and he stepped in.

Before she could speak, he called back to the porter who had brought him up.

"There's a bad escape of gas somewhere in this house," he said.

"I noticed it, sir,"

The porter went prowling along the passage and came back. "It's coming from the room next door," he said.

22

Surefoot knelt and brought his face close to the floor. The smell of gas was overpowering. He tried the handle. The door was fastened on the inside. Repeated knocking produced no response. Stepping back he threw the whole weight of his body against the frame. There was a crash and he fell headlong into the room. The place was so full of gas that he was almost asphyxiated and only staggered out with difficulty. Going into the girl's room, he soaked a towel in water and clapping it over his face ran through to the room and flung open the window. Then, turning his attention to the man who lay on the bed, he put his arm round him and dragged him into the passage.

The man was still breathing. One glance he took at the purple face, and in his astonishment almost dropped the inanimate figure. Leo Moran!

By this time the hotel was aroused. A doctor, who lived on the same floor, came out in pyjamas and an overcoat, and rendered first aid, whilst Surefoot went back into the room.

He switched on the electric light. The gas was still hissing from the burner on the hearth and he turned this off before he opened the window wider. He saw now that elaborate preparations had been made for this near tragedy. There was sticking-plaster down each side of the window. He found it also over the keyhole, and the space between the bottom of the door leading into the bathroom had been stuffed with a towel. Near the bed was a half-glass of whisky and soda. Evidently Moran had been writing. Surefoot took up a half-finished letter. He saw it was addressed to the general manager of the bank for which he had worked.

DEAR SIR,

"I am back in London, and for reasons which I will explain to you, I am living under an assumed name at this hotel. The explanation which I will give I think will satisfy…"

Here the writing ended in a scrawl, as though Moran had been suddenly overcome.

There was a closely typed foolscap sheet on the table, but this Surefoot did not see immediately.

He looked round the room; the first thing that struck him was that the door of a large cupboard stood wide open and on the floor of the cupboard, which was empty, were two muddy footprints. They were unmistakably the prints of goloshes, and he remembered the old pair of goloshes which had been found in the car where Mike Hennessey's body had been discovered. Somebody had been hiding there. Outside it had been raining heavily; the prints were still wet.

He went outside and found that Moran had been carried into another bedroom, where the doctor and the porter were engaged in applying artificial resuscitation. Returning to Moran's room, he remembered the typewritten sheet which lay on the top of other documents and picked it up. He had not read half a dozen words when his jaw dropped in amazement, and he sat down heavily in a chair: for this typewritten statement was a murder confession.

"I, Leopold Moran, am about to say farewell to life, and, before going, I want to make a full statement concerning the killing of three men. The first of these is a man named Tickler.

In some way he had discovered that I was robbing the bank. He had been blackmailing me for months. He knew that under the name of Mr Washington Wirth I was giving parties, and traced me back to a room over a garage which I used to change my clothes and have used on other occasions as a hiding place. He came into this room and demanded a thousand pounds. I gave him a hundred in treasury notes and then persuaded him to let me drive him down to the West End in a cab that was standing in the mews. As he got into the cab I shot him, closed the door, and, driving him down into Regent Street, left the cab on the rank.

The next day I had an interview with Hervey Lyne. He was growing suspicious. I had forged his name to large sums of money and when, at his request, I called on him, I knew that the game was up. I had tried to bribe Binny – his servant – into helping me to keep the old man in the dark, but Binny was either too honest or too foolish to fall in with my suggestions. Binny is one of the straightest men I have ever met. I think he was a fool to himself, but that is neither here nor there.

I knew Hervey Lyne was in the habit of going into Regent's Park every afternoon and he always chose a spot where I could see him. On the afternoon in question, realising that I could see my finish, I shot him from the window with a rifle to which I had fastened a silencer. What made it so easy was that a noisy car was passing at the time. Afterwards I sent a man to Germany under my name and myself stayed in England.

I was afraid of Hennessey, who was also blackmailing me, and I had to silence him. I drove him into the country, and killed him on the Colnbrook Bypass. Before he died he told me that Miss Lane had the bank statement. That night I entered her house and made a search for it, but found nothing.

All the above is true. I am tired of life and am going out with no regret."

It was signed "Leo Moran."

Surefoot read the confession carefully and then began a search of the room for the goloshes. There was no sign of them.

He found Mary Lane in her room, fully dressed.

"You didn't see the face of the man who tried to get into the room?"

She shook her head.

"Did you recognise him in any other way?"

She thought she had and told him.

As far as he could judge, there was a quarter of an hour between the appearance of the man and the arrival of Surefoot: time enough, if it were Moran, to lock himself in his room. He was reaching this conclusion when he saw something on the floor that glistened. Stooping, he picked up a key. It lay very near to the open window. Going back to Moran's room, he scraped away the plaster that covered the keyhole, put in the key, and turned it. There was no doubt now in his mind.

Moran was still unconscious, though the doctor said he was out of danger. Surefoot had sent for two detectives, and, leaving the banker in their charge, he went back to the Yard.

At one o'clock in the morning three Scotland Yard chiefs were called from their beds and hurried to headquarters. To these Surefoot showed the confession.

"It is as clear as daylight," said his immediate chief. "As soon as he is conscious, shoot him into Cannon Row and charge him."

Surefoot said nothing for a moment, but again examined the foolscap sheet.

"It wasn't typewritten in the room, was it?" he asked. "Perhaps there is such a thing as an invisible typewriter, but I've never seen one. And there was no typewriter in the room. And the door was locked on the inside and the key was on the floor in Miss Lane's room. And the tape over the window was on the outside, not on the inside. That was a little error on somebody's part."

He put his hand in his pocket and took out a small bottle containing an amber liquid.

"That's the whisky that I found in the glass on his writing-table — I want it analysed."

"How was Moran dressed when you found him?" asked one of the chief inspectors.

"He had everything on — including his boots," said Surefoot. "And what is more, he was lying with his feet on the pillow — it is not the position I should choose if I were committing suicide. All very rum and mysterious and scientific, but it doesn't impress *me!*"

The Chief Inspector sniffed.

"Nothing impresses you, Surefoot, except good beer. What is your suggestion?"

Surefoot thought for a while.

"Moran's been out this evening – the hall porter saw him come in an hour before he was discovered. The whisky and soda was sent up to his room – the whisky in a glass and the bottle unopened – an hour before that, on his instructions. I've been through the documents I found on his table, and if there's one thing more certain than another, it is that he had no intention of committing suicide. He has come back to buy a lot of outstanding shares in Cassari Oils and to open a London office for the company. He didn't want to call attention to the fact that he was back – it might have upset his plans for getting the shares he wanted. I found all that in a letter he has written to a Turk in Constantinople. I took the liberty of opening it. And he was seeing the general manager of the bank tomorrow – that doesn't look like suicide."

"Well?" asked the three men together when he paused.

"He didn't try to commit suicide. Somebody got into his room whilst he was out – it was easy, for there are two empty rooms that open on to the balcony – and after getting in he hocussed the whisky and hid himself in the cupboard. When the dope took effect he came out, picked up Moran from the floor, and laid him on the bed. He then stuffed up the ventilation of the room and turned on the gas. Then he got out of the window on to the balcony and made the door air-tight and went out through Miss Lane's room – he probably mistook the room for the one through which he had gained admission to Moran's. He must have dropped the key and was coming back for it, when Miss Lane screamed."

"How did he get out of the hotel without the night porter seeing him?"

Surefoot smiled pityingly.

"There are three ways out, but the easiest is down the service stairs and through the kitchen. There is a coffee cook on duty, but it would be easy to avoid him."

He underlined with his thumb nail a few lines of the confession.

"Notice what a good character he gives to Binny. That was a silly thing to do – a child in arms would know that only Binny could have written that statement.

"Binny – the servant!"

Surefoot nodded.

"He's got several other names," he said. "One of them is Washington Wirth. There's the murderer!"

23

The police chief looked at Surefoot in amazement.

"Binny? You mean Lyne's servant?" asked the senior.

"That's what I mean," said Surefoot calmly.

He dived into the inside of his pocket, took out a flat envelope, and produced from this the transcript of the long cable and a blurred photograph.

"This came over the wire," he explained. "It's a picture of the man – London Len was one of his names – who is wanted by the police of New York and Chicago. He worked with three gangs and was lucky to get away with his life. Listen to this."

He put pince-nez on his broad nose and read from one of the cables.

"This man speaks with a very common English accent. He is believed to have been a valet, and his *modus operandi* is to obtain a situation with a wealthy family and to use the opportunity for extensive robberies. On the side he has worked with several booze rackets, is known to be concerned in the killing of Eddie McGean, and is suspected of other killings."

He twisted the photograph round so that the inspectors could see it.

"It's not pretty. It was taken at police headquarters in New York. If you don't know Binny, I'll tell you that is the bird! Even his best friend would recognise him."

Chief Inspector Knowles examined the photograph and whistled softly.

"I know him. I saw him the day you had him up at the Yard, questioning him. Why should he kill the old boy?"

"Because he's been forging his name. It was Miss Lane who put us on to the track, though I was a dummy not to see it myself. All these forgeries were committed on the seventeenth of the month, and she knew, having lived with the old man, that that was the date he paid all his tradesmen's bills. He was in the habit of writing messages on the back of his cheques, mainly of an insulting nature. The one we deciphered said: 'No more Chinese e –.' Miss Lane knew that the old man lived under the impression that tradesmen spent their lives swindling him. It was his belief that nothing but Chinese or imported eggs were sent to him. To keep his egg and butter man up to the scratch, he used to make a note on the back of the cheque when be paid his bill. That was his practice with all tradesmen – Miss Lane has seen most of them: bootmakers, tailors, provision merchants of all kinds. And do you know what they told her?"

Surefoot leaned forward over the table and spoke slowly, tapping his finger on the desk to emphasise each word.

"They told her that two or three years ago Lyne stopped paying by cheque – and paid cash! Binny either used to go round and settle, or send the money by postal order. Do you know what that means? It means that Lyne was going blind, and that the cheques he was signing for the tradesmen were cheques going into Binny's private account. What made it easier for Binny – which is his real name, by the way – was that the old man would never admit that his sight was failing, and in his vanity claimed that he could read as well as the next man. It was easy for Binny, on the seventeenth of the month, to put cheques before his master and pretend they were in settlement of tradesmen's bills, when in reality they were filled in with pencil for the correct amount. I've seen some of them, and under the microscope you can see the pencil marks and the original amounts for which they were drawn. It was easy to rub them out after the signature had been obtained, and to fill them in for the amount Binny happened to require at the time."

"He must have got wind that these investigations were going on, for he went after Miss Lane, and she saved herself by pretending she thought it was Moran. It was that which probably saved her life. When Binny heard her shout out of the window that Moran was trying to break into her room, he thought he'd leave well alone, and quitted. If he'd had any intelligence, he would have known that all her enquiries incriminated, not Moran, but him! But that's the way of 'em – if criminals had any sense they'd never be hanged."

The Chief Inspector pushed the photograph back across the table.

"Where was the murder committed – the murder of Lyne, I mean?"

Surefoot shook his head.

"That's the one thing that puzzles me. It is possible, of course, that he did the shooting just at the moment Dornford's car passed. The 'confession' that he prepared to throw the crime on to Moran – he was a mug to say so many nice things about Binny – almost suggests that this is the case. All the other crimes in this document were committed by Binny in the way he described."

He went back to the hotel to see Moran. There were other aspects of the case which needed elucidation.

Mike Hennessey's death puzzled him. If the manager was blackmailing Binny, there was motive enough. But what could Mike Hennessey know, except that the servant of the day was the magnificent Washington Wirth by night? And why should he blackmail the man who was providing him with a generous income?

There was a very special reason for killing Hennessey: of that he was sure.

Before he left the Yard Surefoot tightened the cords of the net about the man he wanted. Binny had not been seen since the night Mary Lane sent him to Newcastle on a fictitious errand so that she could try the key of the pantry door of Hervey Lyne's house.

The illuminated key was a mystery no longer. Sometimes "Mr Washington Wirth" came back from these little parties of his a little exhilarated. It was necessary that he should change his clothes in the room above the garage, and once or twice, in changing them, he had left his key behind. Possibly he was a methodical man and was in the habit of putting the key on the table. Its phosphorescent quality was added so that, even if he switched off the light, he would not forget this necessary method of gaining admission to Lyne's house.

On the night of Tickler's murder he had forgotten the key and was compelled to break a window to get into the scullery – this had been Mary's theory. She had recognised the key; as a child she had seen it every day. She had sent Binny to the north to give herself the opportunity of testing out her theory. She had nearly lost her life in doing so, for Binny was no fool: he had left the carriage and gone back ahead of her to his lair.

The detective found Leo Moran conscious, but a very unhappy man, for the after-effects of gas poisoning are not pleasant. All that he told Surefoot confirmed what that intelligent officer had already discovered from a perusal of his private correspondence.

Surefoot showed him the "confession," and read portions of it to the astonished man.

"Murder!" said Moran scornfully. "What rubbish! Who has been murdered?"

When Surefoot told him:

"Hervey Lyne? Good God! How perfectly dreadful! When did this happen?"

"The day you went away," said Surefoot.

Moran frowned.

"But I saw him the day I went away, from my window. He was sitting under the tree in the park – when I say 'the tree' I mean the tree he always used as shade. I've seen him there dozens of times. Binny was reading to him."

"What time was this?" asked Surefoot quickly. Moran thought for a while, then gave an approximate hour.

"That must have been ten minutes before he was found dead. It was too far away for you to see whether he was talking?"

Moran nodded.

"When I saw him, Binny was reading to him." Here was unexpected evidence. Moran was probably the only man who had watched that little group in Hervey Lyne's last moments.

"Where was he sitting – Binny, I mean?"

"Where he usually sat," said Leo Moran instantly. "Facing the old man, practically on a level with his feet. I was watching them for some time."

"Did you see Binny walk round to the back of the chair?"

The other hesitated.

"Yes, he did – I remember now. He walked right round the chair. I remember being reminded of how gamblers walk round a chair for luck."

"You saw nothing else – heard nothing?"

Moran stared at him.

"Do you suspect Binny?"

Surefoot nodded. "It isn't a case of suspicion, it's a case of certainty."

Again the sick man taxed his memory.

"I am almost sure I am right in saying that he went round the chair. I didn't hear anything – you mean a shot? No, I did not hear that, nor did I see Binny behaving suspiciously."

Surefoot skimmed through the "confession" again.

"Do you know Binny?"

"Slightly. He was my servant; I dismissed him for stealing. I lost a number of little trinkets."

Smith put his hand in his pocket and took out the silver cigarette case that had been found under the cushion of the car in which Mike Hennessey had ridden to his death.

The banker stretched out his hand eagerly.

"Good Lord, yes! I wouldn't have lost that for a fortune. It's one of the things that were missing. How did you get it?"

In the man's present condition Surefoot decided it was not the moment to tell of the other horror which had been fastened upon him.

"I thought it might be," he said, pocketing the case. "It was obviously an old one and not the kind of case you would use, and certainly not the kind you would put where I found it. It had been polished up for the occasion, too."

"What was the occasion?" asked Moran curiously, but the detective evaded the question.

Moran spoke quite frankly of his own movements. "I was a fool to go off so hurriedly," he confessed, "but I was rather piqued with my directors, who had refused me leave. It was very vital I should be in Constantinople whilst the board of the Cassari Company was being reconstructed. I have very heavy interests in that company, which is now one of the richest oil companies in the world. And, by the way, Miss Lane is a rich lady; the shares I bought from her could not be transferred to me under Turkish law without yet another signature. Legally I have the right to that; morally I haven't; so the stock she transferred, I am transferring back at the price I paid. Which means that she has more money than she can spend in her lifetime." He smiled. "And so have I, for the matter of that," he added.

There was nothing more to be gained from Moran, and Smith left him to sleep off his intolerable headache. Scotland Yard had phoned that Dick Allenby was on his way back from Paris by aeroplane. He reached Croydon at dawn and found a police car waiting to take him to Regent's Park.

As the car drove into Naylors Crescent he saw Surefoot Smith and three plain clothes officers waiting outside the house.

"Sorry to bring you back, but it is necessary that I should make another search of this house, and it is very advisable you should be present."

"Did you find Moran?" asked Dick impatiently. "You got my telephone message – "

Surefoot nodded.

"Did he tell you anything about Binny?"

"Binny's told me quite a lot about himself," said Surefoot grimly. "I haven't interviewed the gentleman, but he left a very illuminating document."

Dick opened the door of the house and they went in. Although it had only been unoccupied for a very short time, it smelt of emptiness and neglect. Hervey Lyne's study had been tidied up after the detective's search. Every corner had been examined, the very floorboards and hearthstone lifted by the police in their vain effort to find a clue. It was unlikely that this apartment would yield any fresh evidence.

They went into the kitchen, where Mary Lane had her unpleasant adventure. Smith had visited the place an hour or two after Mary's escape, had passed through the cupboard door down a flight of steps to the coal cellar. The truckle bed he had found there on his first visit had been removed.

"The queerest thing about Binny is his wife," said Surefoot. "Why he should attach himself, or allow himself to be attached, to this poor drunkard is beyond my understanding. He must have smuggled her away the night Miss Lane came here, and where she is at the moment I'd rather not enquire."

Dick had already expressed his opinion on this matter. He thought it was probable that the woman was not Binny's wife at all. Hervey Lyne invariably advertised for a man and wife. To gain admission to the establishment Binny would not have been above hiring a woman to suit his purpose. This theory was rather supported by the fact that "Mrs Binny" occupied a small, separate room. That she could have been a source of menace to the murderer was unlikely. The evidence of tradesmen had been that she was invariably in a state of fuddle, and that the cooking was done by Binny himself.

24

The bath-chair in which the old man had been found dead occupied a place under the stairs, and to Dick's surprise the detective gave instructions to have it taken into the front room study. Surefoot had always had an uncomfortable feeling that he had not paid sufficient attention to the chair. What he had learned in the past few days made a further examination essential.

Immediately opposite the door of the study there was an alcove in the wall of the passage, and he saw now that this served a useful purpose. Obviously Lyne was in the habit of getting into the bath-chair in the study. Against the lintel of the door, at the height of the wheel's hub, were several scratches and indentations where the hub had touched the wood. But for the fortuitous circumstance of the alcove being so placed, it would have been difficult either to take the chair into the room or bring it out. Surefoot put a detective into the chair and made the experiment of drawing him into the street. The width of the conveyance was only a few inches less than the width of the front door opening and again he found marks on the door posts where the hub had touched. Without assistance he drew the chair into the street. The wheels fitted into the little tramlines which Lyne had had placed for the purpose. The slope was so gentle that it was as easy to pull the laden chair back into the house.

The experiment told him very little. On the day of the murder he had examined every square inch of the vehicle. He ordered it to be put back in the place where it had been found and then continued his search and examination of the house.

"What do you expect to find?" asked Dick.

"Binny," was the terse reply. "This fellow isn't a fool. He has got a hiding place somewhere, and I wish I knew where to look for it." He looked at his watch. "I wonder if I could persuade Miss Lane to come along?"

Dick Allenby took a cab to the hotel, a little doubtful whether after the excitement of the night she would be either physically fit or willing to come to this house of gloom.

He found her in her sitting-room, showing no evidence of the strain she had experienced. Her first question was about Binny.

"No, we haven't found him," said Dick. His voice was troubled. "I am getting terribly worried about you, Mary. This fellow would stop at nothing."

She shook her head.

"I don't think he'll worry me again," she said. "Mr Smith is right: Binny will take no risk that does not bring him profit. As long as he thought he could get the bank statement from me or stop me speaking and telling what I had discovered about the cheques, I think I must have been in terrible danger."

"How did he know you were making enquiries?"

"He knew when I sent him up to the North," she said. "That was a crude little plan, wasn't it?" I under-rated his intelligence and he must have been following me when I was visiting the tradesmen. I had an idea once that I saw him. It was the day I went to Maidstone."

She showed no reluctance in accompanying Dick back to the house. On the way she told him that she had seen Leo Moran in the night and that he was out of danger. There had been a time when the doctors had been doubtful as to whether he would recover.

They reached the house. Surefoot was in the little courtyard at the back. She followed Dick down the few steps that led to the kitchen. She shuddered as she recalled her midnight visit to this sinister little apartment. Even now, in the light of day, it had an unpleasant atmosphere, due, she admitted to herself, rather to her imagination than to unhappy memory. There was the "cupboard" door wide open now and the little door into which she had fitted the replica of the silver key. The kitchen and the adjoining scullery seemed amazingly small. She realised that this was due to the fact that her earliest recollections of the house belonged to childhood when small rooms look large and low articles of furniture unusually high.

Surefoot came in as she was looking around and nodded a greeting.

"Remember this, Miss Lane?"

"Yes." She pointed to the inner kitchen, looking very modern with its lining in white glazed brick. "That's new," she said, and walked in.

The place puzzled her: she missed something, and try as she did she could not recollect what it was. Some feature of the room as she remembered it, was missing. She did not mention her doubts, thinking that memory was playing tricks – a way that memory has.

"You know what this is?" asked Smith.

He had found it in the kitchen drawer: a curious looking instrument rather like a short garden syringe, except that at the end was a rubber cup.

"It is a vacuum pump," explained Smith.

He wetted the edge of the rubber cup, pressed it on the table and, drawing up the piston, lifted the table bodily at one end.

"What's the idea of that? Have you ever seen it before?"

She shook her head.

Surefoot had found some other things: a small pot of dark-green paint and a hardened mass wrapped in oily newspaper.

"Putty," he explained. "I saw it when I was here before. Do you know what it was used for?"

He beckoned her and she followed him into a dark passage. The lamp that had been switched on gave very little light, but Surefoot took a powerful little torch from his pocket and, walking up to the door, stooped and, sending the bright light along the inside of the thick door panel, said: "You see that, and that?"

She saw now a deep circular indentation.

"It was filled with putty and painted over. I thought it was a nut-hole until I started picking out the putty."

"What is it?" she asked wonderingly.

"It is the mark made by a spent bullet," said Smith slowly. "The bullet that killed Hervey Lyne. He was shot in this passage."

25

"It's all based on deduction so far," said Surefoot, "but it is the kind of deduction that I am willing to bet on, and that is saying a lot for me: I don't waste money. Binny had known for some time that the old man was suspecting him and things were getting desperate. He had to do something and do it pretty quickly. The old man was getting suspicious about his bank account. He could not suspect Binny or he would not have told him to send for Moran. Lyne hated bankers and never had an interview unless he couldn't help it. When Binny found he had sent for his bank manager he was in a hole. There was only one thing he could do and that was to get a confederate to pose as a bank manager and that confederate was – "

"Mike Hennessey!" said Dick.

Surefoot nodded.

"I haven't any doubt about that," he said. "When we searched Hennessey's clothes we found a paper containing the identical figures that were on the statement. This could only mean that Binny had supplied him with the figures and that Mike had had to commit them to memory in case the old man questioned him. Obviously the paper had been continuously handled. It was extremely soiled and had been folded and re-folded."

They were in the kitchen and providentially Surefoot had found a big sheet of blotting paper, which he spread on the table, and on which he elaborated his theory as he spoke.

"Moran was never notified and never asked to call. It happened by a coincidence that he was not in his office at the time of the interview. He was, in fact, consulting with the agents of the Cassari Oils. At the time fixed for the appointment Mike came. Hervey Lyne had never seen the bank manager, and even if he had he would not have recognised him for he was nearly blind. He must have said something or done something which left the old man unsatisfied. Lyne was very shrewd. One of his hobbies was working out how he could be swindled and it is possible that he had a doubt in his mind whether the man who called on him was Moran.

"We shall never know what it was that made suspicion a certainty. It may have been something he overheard in the kitchen: there were times when Binny and his so-called wife had unholy rows – I got this from the servants in the next house. He picked up the first piece of paper he could find – it happened to be the bank statement – and wrote the message to you." He nodded at Mary. "I do not think there is any doubt that he was sure that the man who had called that morning was not Moran, and that he suspected Binny of being the villain of the piece and that is why he asked that the police should be sent for. Binny got to know this. Whether the old man charged him at the last moment or said something, we shall only know if Binny tells the truth before he is hanged.

"Binny must have made his plans on the spur of the moment. After he dressed the old man to take him out, he stepped behind him and shot him with a magazine pistol – I dug out the bullet from the door. It is possible that he had no intention of taking him out, but after he found there was very little blood and no sign of a wound, he decided to take the risk. The blue glasses Mr Lyne wore hid his eyes. He was generally half asleep as he was being pulled into the park. Binny got away with it. He even asked a policeman to hold up the traffic to allow the chair to pass."

Surefoot Smith sighed and shook his head in reluctant admiration.

"Think of it! Him sitting there dead, and Binny as cool as a cucumber, reading the news to the dead man."

"Is there a chance of Binny getting out of England?" asked Dick.

Surefoot scratched his nose thoughtfully.

"Theoretically – no, but this man is a play actor, meaning no disrespect to you, Miss Lane. I don't believe in criminals disguising themselves, but this man isn't an ordinary criminal. At the moment he is in London, probably living in a flat which he has rented under another name. He may have two or three of them. He is the sort of man who would be very careful to make all preparations for a getaway. He has got stacks of money, a couple of automatic guns, and the rope ahead of him. He is not going to be taken easily."

"I don't understand him," said Dick, shaking his head. "Why these theatrical parties? Why Mr Washington Wirth?"

"He had to have some sort of swell name and appearance. I will tell you all about the theatrical parties one of these days. He never got the right people there, with all due respect to you, Miss Lane. He wanted ladies wearing thousands of pounds' worth of diamonds. He worked that racket in Chicago: got a big party and held them up, but he never caught on in London and never attracted the money. And you have got to allow for vanity, too. He liked to be a big noise even among little people, again with all due respect to you, Miss Lane."

He picked up the vacuum pump and looked at it.

"I'd like to know what this is for. I think I will take it along with me."

He slipped it into his pocket. They went out after locking all the doors – Dick and the girl to the hotel, and the indefatigable Mr Smith to his Haymarket flat.

An hour passed in that house. There was neither sound nor movement, until an oblong strip of glazed brickwork began to open like a door, and Binny, wearing rubber overshoes, came cautiously into the kitchen, gun in hand. He listened, went swiftly and noiselessly into the passage, up the stairs from room to room before he came back to the front door and slipped a bolt in its place. Returning to the kitchen, he laid his gun on the table and passed his hand over his unshaven chin. His unprepossessing face creased in a smile which was not pleasant to see.

"Vanity, eh?" he said.

It was the one thing the detective had said that had infuriated him.

Binny stood by the table, his unshapely head sunk in thought, his fingers playing mechanically with the long-barrelled automatic that lay at his hand.

Vanity! That had hurt him. He hated Surefoot Smith; from the first time he had seen him he had recognised in this slow, ponderous, unintelligent-looking man a menace to his own security and life. And he had offended him beyond all pardon. Whatever anybody could say about this amazing man, his love of the theatre was genuine. Association with its people was the breath of his nostrils. His first defalcations were made for the purpose of financing a play that ran only a week. He himself was no bad actor. He would require all his skill and genius to escape from the net which was being drawn about him. He went back through the narrow door into a room that was smaller than the average prison cell.

It was narrow and long. On the floor was a mattress where he had slept, and at the foot of the "bed" was a small dressing-table, beneath which were two suitcases. He took one of these out and unlocked it. On the top lay a flat envelope containing three passports, which he brought into the kitchen. Pulling up a chair to the table, he examined each one carefully. He had made his preparations well. The passports were in names that Surefoot Smith had never heard of and there was no resemblance to him in the three photographs attached to each passport. Fastened to one by a rubber band was a little packet of railway tickets. One set would take him to the Hook of Holland, another to Italy. He could change his identity three times on the journey.

From a bulging hip pocket he took a thick pad of banknotes: French, English, German. He took another pad from a concealed pocket in his coat, a third and fourth, until there was a great pile of money on the table.

For a quarter of an hour he sat contemplating his wealth thoughtfully, then, going back into his little hiding place, he carried out a mirror and a small shaving set and began carefully to make his preparations.

Vulgar grease paints, however convincing they might look on the stage, would have no value in the light of day. He poured a little anatto into a saucer, diluted it and sponged his face carefully, using a magnifying mirror to check the effects.

For the greater part of two hours he laboured on his face and head; then, stripping to his underclothes, he began to dress, having first deposited his money in satchels that were attached to his belt, which was passed round his waist. The contents of the two cases he turned out, for he had examined them very carefully the day before. He could not afford to carry any other baggage than the two automatics and half a dozen spare magazines, which he disposed about his person.

He chose the lunch hour, and then only after a long scrutiny of the street from the study window. The servants might see him, but the chances were that they would be preparing or serving the meal either to their employers or to themselves. It was the hour, too, when no tradesmen were delivering, and the only risk was that Surefoot Smith had left somebody to watch the house. That had to be taken.

He unbolted the front door, turned the handle, and stepped out. As he reached the Outer Circle he saw something that made him set his jaw. A slatternly looking woman was walking unsteadily on the other side of the street. He recognised her as the miserable companion of the past four years, the half-witted drunkard who had shared the kitchen with him. She did not recognise him, and it mattered little even if Surefoot saw her. He had turned her out the previous day with instructions to go back to Wiltshire, where he had found her, and had given her enough money to keep her for a year.

He plodded on, looking back occasionally to see if he were followed. He dared not risk a bus. A taxi would be almost as dangerous. To drive a car in his present disguise would be to attract undesirable attention.

In the Finchley Road there was a block of buildings, the ground floor of which was shops. Above these was a number of apartments occupied by good middle-class tenants. The corner of the block, however, had been reserved for offices and this had a private self-operated elevator.

Binny went into the narrow passage unchallenged, pressed the button, and had himself carried onto the third floor. Almost opposite the lift, at an angle of the wall, was a door inscribed: "The New Theatrical Syndicate." He unlocked the door and went in. The office consisted of one medium-sized room and a small cloakroom. It was furnished plainly and had the appearance of being very rarely used. Except for a desk and a table there was no evidence of its business character.

He shot a little bolt in the door, took off the long coat he wore, and sat down in the comfortable chair. In one of the drawers there was a small electric kettle, which he filled in the wash-place. He brewed himself a cup of coffee, and this, with some biscuits he found in a tin box, in the second drawer, comprised his lunch.

The getaway was going to be simple. His real luggage was in the cloakroom at Liverpool Street. Everything was simple, and yet –

Binny could have written a book on the psychology of criminals. He was a cold-blooded, reasoning killer, who never made the stupid errors of other criminals. It was a great pity that he had made the appalling mistake of going back to find the key and had attracted the girl's attention. Otherwise, Leo Moran would have been dead and there would be no proof that the confession, which Binny had typed out so industriously, was not true in every detail.

He had planned it all so carefully: he had intended dropping the key just on the inside of the locked door and had put it in his pocket and had forgotten it. A little slip that had messed up his artistic plan. Reason, which had determined his every action, told him to slip out of London quietly that night and trust to his native genius for safety. But that something which is part of the mental makeup of criminal minds clamoured for the spectacular. It would be a great stunt to leave London with one crushing exploit which would make him the talk of the world. In his imagination he could see the headlines in the newspapers.

"SUREFOOT SMITH LEFT DEAD AND THE
MURDERER ESCAPED!"

171

"SUREFOOT SMITH, THE GREAT CATCHER OF
MURDERERS, WAS HIMSELF CAUGHT!"

The fantastic possibilities took hold of him. His mind began
to work, not towards safety, but in the direction of pleasing
sensationalism, and he did not realise that the charge of vanity which
he so resented was being justified with every mental step he took
towards vengeance.

26

Dick Allenby and Mary were lunching at the Carlton, and they were talking about things which ordinarily would have absorbed her.

"You are not listening," he accused her, and she started.

"Wasn't I?" She was very penitent. "Darling, I was thinking of something else. Isn't that a terrible confession? I don't suppose any other girl ever listened to a proposal of marriage with her mind on a nasty old kitchen in an unpleasant little house."

He laughed.

"If you could bring that mind of yours from the drab realities to the idyllic possibilities, I should be a very happy man." And then, curiously: "You mean Hervey Lyne's house? What's worrying you?"

"The kitchen," she said promptly. "There was something there, Dick – I can't think what it was – something I missed, and it is worrying me. I have a dim recollection that the poor old man told me he was having the kitchen rebuilt. I remember him saying what a wonderful fellow Binny was, because he was superintending the operations and saving him a lot of money." She fingered her chin. "There was a dresser," she said thoughtfully. "Of course, that's gone. And a horrid little sink of brown earthenware, and – "

She stopped suddenly and stared at him, wide eyed.

"The larder!" she gasped. "Of course, that's what it was! There was a larder and a door in the wall leading to it. What has happened to the larder?"

He shook his head helplessly.

"I haven't been terribly interested in larders," he began, but she arrested his flippancy.

"Don't you remember Mr Smith said as we were leaving the house that he was sure Binny had a hiding place somewhere? I am sure that's it – on the right hand side as you go in."

Dick Allenby laughed.

"On the right hand side as you go into the kitchen there is a solid brick wall," he said, but she shook her head.

"I am sure there is something behind it. I remember now, when I went into the courtyard to try the key I noticed that there had been no change in the exterior. There must be a space there. Dick, Providence is with us."

She was looking towards the entrance. Surefoot Smith was there, very disconsolate. He caught her eye and nodded. Obviously she was not the person he wanted to see, for he continued his scrutiny of the room. She caught his eye again and beckoned him. He came forward reluctantly.

"You haven't seen the Deputy Assistant Commissioner, have you? I'm lunching with him – he is paying for it. He said half-past one." He looked at his watch. "It is nearly two. We've pinched Binny's wife, by the way; one of our men picked her up on the Outer Circle, but she's got nothing to say."

"I've found the hiding place!" Mary blurted the news, and Surefoot Smith became instantly alert.

"Binny's?" he asked quickly. "In the house you mean?"

She told him breathlessly of her theory. He slapped his knee.

"You're right, of course – the vacuum pump. I wondered what he used it for. If there was a door – and it was an easy job to make a door on glazed brick – he could not have had handles, could he? The only way he could get it open would be by sticking the vacuum on the surface of the brick to give him a grip. I have got the pump at the Yard, and the Commissioner can wait."

He went out of the room, and half an hour later Hervey Lyne's little house was surrounded. Surefoot came into the hall, pistol in hand, went quickly into the kitchen and examined the white wall. There was no sign of a door. He fastened the vacuum to the smooth surface and pulled, but, to his chagrin, nothing happened. The strength of two detectives failed to move the door. He moved the position of the pump from time to time, and at the fifth attempt he was rewarded. The slightest pull drew a brick from the wall. It ran on a steel guide, and dropped over in front, leaving an oblong aperture which was hollow.

He put his hand inside and felt a steel handle, which he turned and pulled. The door swung open and he was in Binny's hiding place. The disordered heap of clothes on the floor, the shaving mirror thrown down on the bed, told their own tale. There was greater significance, however, in the saucer he found in the sink. It was still yellow with the annatto colouring which Binny had used.

Surefoot Smith looked at it for a long time, and then: "I think there is going to be serious trouble," he said.

Surefoot Smith hurriedly turned over the clothes and articles which had been emptied from the suitcase, but he found nothing to give him the slightest clue to Binny's intentions. One thing was certain: he had been in his hiding place and had heard all that had happened that morning. Surefoot had the door shut and himself listened to conversation in the kitchen, and although he could not catch every word he was satisfied that Binny had heard enough.

The annatto in the saucer was a very slight and possibly useless clue. It told him to look for a yellow faced man, and this might or might not be a useful guide to the searchers.

The fugitive had left nothing else behind. Surefoot searched diligently, crawling over the floor with his eyes glued to the tiled flooring for some sign of crepe hair. He expected this stage-mad murderer to have attempted some sort of theatrical disguise, but his search failed to reveal anything that left a hint as to what that disguise might be.

The only piece of incriminating evidence which Binny had left behind was the sealed magazine of an automatic pistol, and, since this could not have been overlooked, the detective surmised that the magazine had been left because the man was carrying as many as he conveniently could.

Another discovery, which, at an earlier stage, would have been invaluable, was a soiled white glove, obviously the fellow of that which Surefoot had found in Mr Washington Wirth's changing-room.

"You never know," said Surefoot as he handed over the glove to his subordinate. "Juries go mad sometimes, and a little thing like that might convince 'em – keep it."

The larder had evidently been used as a sleeping-room. Although the bed was on the floor, and the apartment itself was bare, Binny had often found this a convenient retreat. Very little daylight came through the small window near the ceiling, and apparently he kept that closed most of the time; it was covered with a square of oilcloth.

Before he left Surefoot tried the experiment of having the clothes packed in the suitcase. He found, as he had expected, that there was only sufficient to fill one. He was satisfied, too, that some of the clothes he had found had been recently changed by Binny, and the conclusion he reached was that one of the suitcases had contained the disguise which the murderer wore when he left the house.

He sent his men on missions of enquiry up and down the street, but nobody had seen Binny leave – he had chosen the hour well. Later he widened the circle of enquiry, but again was unsuccessful.

He found Mary Lane and her fiancé waiting patiently in the palm court of the Canton, and reported his discoveries.

"If only I'd thought of it before!" she said ruefully.

Surefoot Smith's smile was not altogether unpleasant.

"Either you or I or all of us would have been dead," he said grimly. "That bird carries a young arsenal, and your bad memory probably saved us a whole lot of unpleasantness."

"Do you think he was there?"

He nodded.

"There's no doubt about it."

"He'll get away, then?" asked Dick.

Surefoot rubbed his chin irritably.

"I wonder if that would be a good thing or a bad thing?" he said. "He may try to leave today – all the ports are being watched, and every single passenger will be under inspection. The only person who can pass on and out to a ship leaving this coast tonight is a baby in arms – and we search even him!"

He drew his chair closer to the table and leaned across, lowering his voice.

"Young lady," he said, and he was very serious, "you know what rats do when they're in a corner – they bite! If this man can't get out of England by walking out or shooting himself out, he's coming back to the cause of all his trouble. I'm one, but you're another. Do you know where I should like to put you?"

She shook her head, for the moment incapable of speech. She was shocked, frightened a little, if she had confessed it. Binny was on her nerves, more than she would admit. She felt her heart beating a little faster, and when she spoke she was oddly breathless.

"Do you really think that?" And then, forcing a smile: "Where would you put me?"

"In Holloway Prison." He was not joking. "It's the safest place in London for an unmarried woman who's living around in hotels and flats; and if I could find an excuse for putting you there for seven days I would."

"You're not serious?" said Dick, troubled.

Surefoot nodded.

"I was never more serious in my life. He may get out of the country; I don't think it's possible that he will. If Miss Lane had not remembered the larder I should not take the precautions I am taking tonight. The doors out of England are locked and barred, unless he's got an ocean-going motor-boat somewhere on the East Coast, and I have an idea that he hasn't."

Then, abruptly:

"Where are you staying tonight?"

Mary shook her head.

"I don't know. I think at the hotel – "

"You can't stay there." He was emphatic. "I know a place where you could stay. It wouldn't have the conveniences of an hotel, but you'd have a decent bed and security." There was a new police station in the north-west of London, which had married quarters above it, and one of these was occupied by a woman whose husband, a detective sergeant, had gone to Canada to bring back a fugitive from justice.

"I know this woman; she's a decent sort, and she'll give you a bed, if you wouldn't mind sleeping there."

She agreed very meekly. Indeed, she had a sense of relief that he had found such a simple solution.

Surefoot Smith had a queer sixth sense of danger. He had been concerned in many murder cases, had dealt with scores of desperate men who would not have hesitated to kill him if they had had the opportunity. He had known cunning men and a few clever criminals, but Binny was an unusual type. Here was a killer with no regard for human life. Murder to him was not a desperate expedient – it was part of a normal method.

There was a long conference at Scotland Yard and new and urgent telegrams were sent to all parts of the country insisting upon the dangerous character of the wanted man. Ordinarily the English police do not carry firearms, but in this case, as the messages warned a score of placid chief constables, it would be an act of suicide to accost the wanted man unless the police officer whose duty it was to arrest him was prepared to shoot.

Scotland Yard has a record of all projected sailings, and neither from Liverpool nor Greenock was there any kind of boat due to leave in the next thirty-six hours.

Binny's avenue of escape must be the Continent. Strong detachments of CID men were sent to reinforce the watchers at Harwich, Southampton, and the two Channel ports. And yet, when these preparations were completed, Surefoot Smith had a vague feeling of uneasiness and futility. Binny was in London, and he was too clever a man even to think of leaving, unless he was ignorant that his hiding place had been discovered. There was no reason why he should not be. It was hardly likely that he had a confederate.

At five o'clock Surefoot made an exasperating discovery: he was strolling in Whitehall when he saw a newspaper placard: "WANTED MURDERER'S SECRET HIDING PLACE." He bought a paper and saw, conspicuously displayed on the front page, a long paragraph headed: "Secret Chamber in Hervey Lyne's House." Surefoot swore softly and read on:

"This afternoon Inspector Smith of Scotland Yard, accompanied by a number of detectives, made a further search of the house of Hervey Lyne – the victim of the Regent's Park murder. The police remained on the premises for some time. It is understood that in the course of their investigations a little room, which they had previously overlooked, was discovered and entered, and unmistakable evidence secured that this secret chamber had been used as a hiding place by the servant Binny, for whom the police have been searching…"

Surefoot Smith read no further. It was a waste of time wondering who had given away the information to the Press. Possibly some young detective who had been engaged in the search and who was anxious to pass on this sensational discovery. To bring home this indiscretion was a matter that could be left till later. In the meantime Binny knew if he were to read the newspapers.

Oddly enough, Binny did not see the paragraph, and had already made up his mind as to the course he would pursue.

At eight o'clock that night Surefoot called at Mary Lane's hotel and escorted her to the plain but very comfortable lodgings he had secured for her.

He had a talk with the inspector on duty, but asked for no guard. She was safe. Binny would be a bold man to show himself abroad, and he certainly would not walk into a police station.

At half-past nine that night Surefoot returned to Scotland Yard and read the reports which had come in. The boat train from Liverpool Street had been carefully combed. There was no sign of Binny or anybody who might have been Binny. Every passport had been examined before the train pulled out and, as an act of precaution, the railway platform had been cleared of friends who had gathered to see off the passengers before the officer in charge had given the station master the "All right."

A similar course was being followed at Waterloo, where the police were watching and searching the trains for Havre. It was too early to hear from the sea ports.

Binny was an expert chauffeur. It was hardly likely that he would get out of London by train if he intended leaving London.

27

The detective left the Yard a few minutes after eleven, and, turning to his left, walked towards Blackfriars. To Surefoot Smith that long ribbon of pavement which runs without a break from Scotland Yard to Savoy Hill was a garden of thought. At headquarters somebody with a florid mind had christened it his "Boulevard of Cogitation." Summer or winter, rain or fine, Surefoot Smith found here the solution of all his problems. Men had been hanged, swindlers had been sent down to the shades, very commonplace happenings had assumed a sinister importance, and, by contrast, seemingly guilty men and women had had their innocence established in the course of Surefoot Smith's midnight recreation.

There were very few pedestrians at this hour of the night. The courting couples, for some strange reason, chose the better lighted river side of the road. Cars flashed past occasionally. There was an irregular procession of street cars at long intervals, and once an occasional night hawk shuffled along the kerbside in search of a stray cigarette end.

Near one of the entrances to the Embankment Gardens a saloon car was drawn up by the kerb. Glancing inside, more from habit than curiosity, Surefoot saw the figure of a woman sitting, and continued his stroll.

He paced on, turning over the question of Binny in his mind. The greater problem was solved; the more dangerous and delicate business of effecting the man's arrest had yet to be accomplished. He was uneasy, which was not usual. Surefoot Smith was a great dreamer. He visualised the most fantastic possibilities, and because he allowed his thoughts the fullest and widest range, he was more successful than many of his fellows. For there is this about dreaming, that it throws the commonplace possibilities into sharp relief, and it is on the commonplace possibilities that most detectives rely.

He turned on his tracks at Savoy Hill and walked slowly back towards the Yard. By this time the reports would be coming in from the coast, though it was still a little too early for any but Southampton, where an extra vigilance was being exercised. A German–American liner, which was due at that port that night, was taking in passengers for Hamburg, and this fact had necessitated sending a second batch of watchers to the port.

He saw the car still standing by the side of the road. It was no great distance from the Lost Property Office and it was likely that the lady had sent her chauffeur in search of something she had left behind her in a cab in the course of the day. As he drew near her he saw that the woman was standing by the open door of the machine – a middle-aged lady, he gathered by her plumpness.

To his surprise she addressed him in a high-pitched voice.

"I wonder if you could fetch a policeman for me?"

A staggering request to make of one of the recognised heads of Scotland Yard.

"What's wrong?" asked Surefoot Smith.

She stepped aside from the door.

"My chauffeur," she said. "He has come back rather the worse for drink, and I can't get him out of the car."

A drunken chauffeur is an offence to all good policemen. Surefoot opened the door wider and peered in.

He saw nothing, heard nothing, felt nothing. His consciousness of life went out like a snuffed candle.

28

His head was aching terribly. He tried to move his hands and found movement restricted. He did not realise why for a long time.

The car was moving with great rapidity, far beyond the legalised speed limit. There were no lights. By the whir of the wheels he guessed he was on a newly made road. It was queer that this fact should have appeared so important to him. He could remember nothing, knew nothing, except that he was lying curled up on the floor of a motor-car which was moving rapidly and smoothly. Then he stopped thinking again for a long time and was glad of the unconsciousness which obliterated this throbbing head of his.

The car was now bumping over an uneven surface. It was that which roused him to consciousness. He blinked up, tried to raise himself, felt gingerly along his wrists and recognised the shape of the handcuffs – his own; he always carried an unauthorised pair in his coat pocket. Unauthorised, because they were not of the regulation type – they were American handcuffs which were so much easier to put on – a tap on the wrist and the D swung round and was fast.

Somebody had handcuffed him. Somebody had tied his legs together with a silk scarf. He could feel it, but he could not reach the knot. And then he remembered the woman and the car and the drunken chauffeur who was not there.

The car was bumping painfully. It seemed to be passing over a ploughed field or, at best, a cart track. It was the latter, he found when the car stopped.

A little while later the door was pulled open; he saw the outlines of the "woman" and knew exactly who she was.

There was a little cottage a few yards away; one of those monstrous little boxes of red brick and tiling that disfigure the countryside since the war. His coat collar was gripped and he was jerked out into the road, falling on his knees.

"Get up, you –," hissed a voice, and what followed was not ladylike.

He was half-dragged and half-pushed towards the cottage; the door was flung open and he was thrust into a dark interior. It smelt of drying mortar and plaster and new wood. He guessed it was unfurnished. He waited awhile. The door was locked on the inside and he was again urged forward into a room so completely dark that he knew the window was shuttered. He fell on the floor. It was amazing that he walked at all with his legs bound, as they were, with the silk scarf.

As he lay there, a match spluttered, there was a tinkle of an oil lamp chimney being taken off, and presently the room was illuminated by the soft glow of a kerosene lamp. The only articles of furniture in the room were two sofas, a chair, and a kitchen table. Wooden shutters covered the window, as he had suspected. There were neither hangings nor curtains of any description, and the table was innocent of cloth.

His captor pulled the chair forward, sat down, his hands on his knees, and surveyed him.

Surefoot would never have recognised this yellow-faced old woman with a grey wig and a long fur coat. The wig was now a little askew – it gave him a comical but terrible appearance. He was sensitive to ridicule, took off the wig and hat with one movement and appeared even more grotesque with his bald head and his yellow face.

"Got you," said Binny huskily.

He was grinning, but there was no merriment in that smile.

"Mr Surefoot Smith is not so sure on his feet after all."

The jest seemed to amuse him, and then, as though conscious of the attitude which the situation demanded, he assumed that affected mincing tone which had belonged to Mr Washington Wirth.

"I built this little place a couple of years ago. I thought it might be useful, but I haven't been here for a long time. I am leaving the country. Perhaps you would like to buy it, Mr Smith? It's an excellent retreat for a professional gentleman who wishes to be quiet, and you are going to be very quiet!"

From his pocket he took an automatic pistol and laid it on the table beside him, and, stooping down, he lifted Surefoot and sat him in a corner of the room. Bending down, he unfastened the sagging silk scarf about his ankles and jerked off the detective's shoes, throwing them into another corner of the room. He hesitated a second, then loosened Surefoot's collar.

"You are not hurt, my dear Mr Smith," he remarked. "A rubber truncheon applied to the back of the neck does not kill. It is, I admit, very uncomfortable. There was once a copper in Cincinnati who tried that treatment on me. It was two months before I was well enough to shoot him. You didn't know of my little retreat?"

Surefoot's mouth was dry, his head was whizzing, but he was entirely without fear, though he realised his case was a desperate one.

"Oh yes, I did, Binny," he said. "This place is about a hundred yards from the Bath Road near Taplow. You bought the ground four years ago, and paid a hundred and fifty pounds for it."

For a second Binny was thrown off his balance.

"This house was searched last week by my police officers, and is now under the observation of the Buckinghamshire police. You have got another cottage of a similar character in Wiltshire."

"Oh, indeed?"

Binny was completely taken aback. He was rattled too. Surefoot saw this and pushed home his advantage.

"What's the good of being a fool? We have got no evidence against you for murder. The only evidence is that you have forged Hervey Lyne's cheques. The worst that can happen to you is a seven stretch."

Again he put his finger upon the one great doubt which obsessed the man.

"You may get an extra year for this," said Surefoot, "but what's a year? Get me some water. There's a kitchen just behind this room. Let the tap run: the water was rusty when I was here last week. There's a tin cup on the dresser."

The instinct to obey is stronger than the instinct to command. Binny went out and returned with the tin cup and put it to the detective's lips.

"Now take these handcuffs off and we'll have a little talk. Why didn't you bring Mike Hennessey here instead of – " He realised his colossal error as soon as the words were spoken.

Binny stepped back with a snarl.

"Don't want me for murder, eh? You double-crossing busy! I will show you what I want you for."

His hand moved towards the gun on the table. Binny took up the pistol and examined it carefully.

"I have always wanted to tell you where you get off, Smith – " he began.

"Your wish has come true," said Surefoot coolly. "But you'd better work fast."

"I'll work fast enough," said the other grimly.

He slipped the gun into his pocket, picked up the scarf, and retied his prisoner's ankles.

He then took off his fur coat and relieved himself of his woman's garments. From a theatre trunk he retrieved an old suit, which he put on.

Surefoot Smith watched him interestedly.

"I gather you have some hard work to do?" he said.

"Pretty hard," said the other, and added significantly: "The ground here is fairly soft. You don't get down to clay till you have dug six feet."

If he expected to terrify his captive he was disappointed.

"Why not let me do it?" said Smith. "You are fat and out of condition. Digging my own grave is a hobby of mine."

For a second Binny seemed to be considering this suggestion.

"No, I'll do it," he said, "fat or not fat."

"Why bother?" Surefoot's voice was almost airy. "As soon as I am missing they will search here and in Wiltshire. I gather your object is to leave no trace. You are not sure now whether we could convict you for murder, are you? If you kill a police officer you are certain to be hanged. Every man in Scotland Yard will turn out to find evidence against you. People who were sleeping in their beds will swear that they saw you cosh me."

He libelled the best police force in the world without shame.

"You might get away with Hennessey," Surefoot went on, "and old Lyne and Tickler, but you could not get away with me. They will come along and search this ground, which, if I remember rightly, is grass-grown, and unless you do a little bit of artistic turfing they will find me and that will be the finish of you."

Binny paused at the door and turned with an ugly grin on his face.

"I used to know a copper who talked like you, but he talked himself into hell, see?"

He went out and closed the door behind him.

Surefoot Smith sat, thinking very hard. He made an effort to break the single link that bound the two cuffs together. It was certainly a painful process, probably impossible. By drawing up his legs and separating them at the knees he could reach the trebly knotted silk scarf. It was difficult, but he succeeded in loosening one knot, and was at work on the second when he heard the man returning along the bare boards of the passage.

Binny was finding his task more difficult than he had anticipated. His face was wet with perspiration. He groped in the trunk, took out a bottle of whisky, and, removing the patent top, took a long drink.

"Is it courage or strength you're looking for?" asked Surefoot.

"You'll see," growled the other, glaring down at the helpless man malignantly.

The butts of two automatics stuck out of his trousers pockets. Surefoot eyed them longingly.

Binny was half-way to the door when a thought struck him, and he turned back and examined the knots of the scarf.

"Oh, you've undone one, have you. We'll see about that."

Again he searched the trunk and found a length of cord. He slipped it round the link of the handcuffs and knotted the cord firmly behind the detective's neck, so that his hands were drawn up almost to his chin.

"You look funny – almost as if you were praying!" remarked Binny. "I shan't keep you long."

He went out of the room on this promise.

Sprawling there helplessly, Surefoot heard the hoot of cars as they passed. He was, he knew, about a hundred yards from the main road, but it was a road along which, day and night, traffic was continually passing.

The possibility that the Buckinghamshire police would search this little cottage was very remote, unless somebody at Scotland Yard had a brainwave that this was the most likely place to which the prisoner would be taken. But Scotland Yard might not even miss him. He was an erratic man; when he was engaged in an important case he would absent himself from headquarters for days together, leaving his chiefs fuming. The search would not begin until Binny was well out of the country.

He watched the smoky oil lamp burning; the flame had been turned on too high and one side of the glass chimney was smoked.

Binny was out for a getaway; he would leave no traces. Even the murder would not be committed in the house.

Half an hour, an hour passed, and he heard the heavy feet of the man coming for him, and knew that the hour was at hand.

29

Scotland Yard had missed Surefoot Smith in the sense that the negative reports which had been taken to his room had not been read or attended to. The fact that they were negative would have justified the officer on duty accepting the situation, but for the peculiar conscientiousness of a young police officer who reported to the station at Cannon Row, which is part of Scotland Yard, that a blue saloon car, driven by a woman, had disregarded his stop signal at the junction of Westminster Bridge and the Embankment, and had driven on the wrong side of the road. He called on it to stop, and, when that failed, had taken its number.

Ordinarily the question of a technical offence of this character would have been left over till the morning, but whilst he was making his statement a Member of Parliament came into the station to report the loss of a blue saloon car, which had been taken from the front of his club in Pall Mall. It had been standing on a rank, against all traffic rules, and he had actually been a witness of the theft.

"It was a man dressed as a woman," was his startling conclusion.

"What makes you think that, sir?" asked the inspector in charge.

"As he got in, the top of the car, which has a very low body, knocked his hat off. It was a bald-headed man with a yellow face like somebody suffering from jaundice."

The inspector sat bolt upright. All England was looking for a bald-headed man with a jaundiced face, and in a few moments the wires were humming.

Again it was a traffic policeman who supplied information, and again it was Binny's anxiety to make a quick run out of London that betrayed him. He had been held up near Heston, where a tramline crosses the main arterial road. He narrowly escaped collision with the tram and the car skidded. The policeman walked across the road to examine the licence of the driver, whose engine had stopped. The policeman distinctly saw a stout woman driver, but before he could ask a question the engine had been restarted and the car moved on. This must have happened in the second period of Surefoot's unconsciousness.

It was not until an hour and a half after the enquiry had been sent out that the traffic policeman's report was received. By this time a "hurry up" call for Surefoot had failed to locate him. Moreover, he had left on his table at Scotland Yard a half-finished sheet of notes.

Now Surefoot never in any circumstances left his notes behind him; and another significant fact was that he had not handed the key of his room to the officer at the door, a practice which he invariably followed, however hurried might be his departure.

His habit of taking a walk was common knowledge. He had been seen walking towards Savoy Hill. The policeman on duty at the foot of the hill had also seen him turn back. Then somebody remembered the blue motor-car that had been standing by the side of the road.

By the time these enquiries had been completed every detective in Scotland Yard had been assembled on the instructions of the hastily summoned chief.

"He may be heading for the coast. What is more likely is that he's on his way to one of those houses of his," said the Chief Constable. "Get the Buckinghamshire and Salisbury police on the phone, and, to make absolutely sure, send squad cars right away to both places."

One of the first people who had been interrogated was Dick Allenby. It was known that Surefoot was a friend of his, and Surefoot was an inveterate gossiper, who loved nothing better than to sit up till three in the morning with a friendly and sympathetic audience. Dick Allenby's arrival at the Yard coincided with the departure of the first squad car for Salisbury.

"We may be chasing moonbeams," said the Chief Constable; "very likely old Surefoot will turn up in about a quarter of an hour, but I am taking no unnecessary risks."

"But he would never get bluffed," said Dick scornfully.

The Chief shook his head.

"I don't know. This fellow has had a pretty hectic experience in America, and it will not be the first person he has taken for a ride in this country."

Of one thing he was sure – that the threat of a revolver would not have induced Surefoot to get into that car.

He looked at his watch; it was half-past one, and he shook his head.

"I wish the night were over," he said.

From that remark Dick sensed all that the other feared.

Surefoot Smith had less than half a minute to do his thinking and to decide on one of the dozen plans – most of them impracticable – that were spinning in his mind.

The door opened slowly and Binny came in. He wiped his forehead on a big handkerchief he took out of his pocket, and sat down.

"You will come a little walk with me, my friend," he said pleasantly.

He took the bottle from the table, swallowed a generous drink, and wiped his mouth. Stooping, he untied the scarf that bound Surefoot's ankles and jerked him to his feet.

Surefoot Smith rose unsteadily. His head was swimming, but the terrific nature of the moment brought about his instant recovery. Binny was standing by the door, fingering his gun. He had fixed to the end of the barrel an egg-shaped object, the like of which Surefoot had never seen before, and he found himself wondering how Dick Allenby, who was interested in silencers and who had asserted so often that a silencer could not be used on an automatic, because of the backfire, would reconcile this freakish thing with his theories.

Surefoot walked to the table and stood, resting his manacled hands on its deal surface.

"Saying a prayer or something?" mocked Binny.

"You don't want anybody to know I have been here, do you? You don't want to leave any trace, and that's why you don't kill me in this room?"

"That's the idea," said the other cheerfully.

"If you had a few hundred people rushing in this direction and asking questions, that would spoil your plan, wouldn't it?"

Binny's eyes narrowed.

"What's the idea?" he demanded.

He took one step towards his prisoner, when Surefoot lifted the lamp and flung it into the open hamper. There was a crash as the glass reservoir broke, a flicker of light, and then a huge flame shot up towards the ceiling.

Binny stood, paralysed to inaction, and in the next moment Surefoot had flung himself upon the man. He drove straight at Binny's face with his clenched hands. The man ducked and the blow missed him. Something exploded in the detective's face; he felt the sting of the powder and heard an expelled cartridge "ting" against the wall.

He struck again, striving to bring the steel handcuffs on to the man's head. Binny twisted aside, but did not wholly escape the impact of the shock. The gun fell from his hand on to the floor.

The room was now a mass of flames; the fire had licked through the thin plaster of the wall and the laths were burning like paper. The atmosphere was thick with acrid smoke, the heat already intolerable.

Again Surefoot struck and again Binny dodged. Surefoot had kicked the pistol out of reach – kicked it into the mass of flames that were spurting from the bottom of the canvas-covered trunk. The door was open and Binny darted out of the room, trying to close it after him, but Smith's shoulders were in the way. Jerking the door wider, he stumbled into the passage and hurled himself at the murderer.

The only hope was to keep at close quarters. Binny had another pistol, had it half out of his pocket, when Surefoot pinned him against the hot wall, and, bracing his feet, exerted all his strength to crush him there. In this position it was impossible to hit the man. In the half-light he saw Binny reaching out towards the front door and edged him nearer to facilitate his task. As the door was flung open and the air came rushing in, the hum of the fire became a roar; flames were flung out like red and yellow banners whipped by the wind.

Binny was trying to pull himself clear of the hands that held him by the singlet; striving desperately to pull out his second pistol. His breath was coming in shrill whistles; he was frightened, had lost all his old reserve of courage. He wriggled desperately to escape the pressure of the heavy figure that was jammed against him, and at last, by a superhuman effort, he succeeded, and darted through the door, Surefoot behind him. His gun was out now and he fired. The detective hurled himself on his man and brought him down. He was up in a second and was running towards the back of the house.

The flames were coming from the roof. The countryside for a hundred yards was almost as light as day. Surefoot, handcuffed as he was, flew in pursuit; and then suddenly Binny turned, and this time his aim was deliberate. Surefoot Smith knew that there was no hope now. The man who covered him was a dead shot, and was within half a dozen paces of him.

In desperation he sprang forward. His feet touched air, and he was falling, falling…

He heard the shot, wondered dimly if this was death, and was brought to the realisation that he was still alive by the impact of his body at the bottom of the hole into which he had fallen. He realised at once what had happened: Binny had been busy all that night preparing this hiding place for his crime, but had missed falling into the hole.

He struggled to his feet, bruised and aching, heard a second shot and looked up. There was a third and fourth. An authoritative voice was challenging somebody. Then he heard his own name called, and shouted. A man's face loomed over the edge of the pit. It was his own sergeant. They brought him up to the top.

"He won't get away," said the detective to whom Surefoot addressed a gasping enquiry.

"Which way did he go, and where is his car?"

He was weary, aching from head to foot, bruised and scratched, but for the moment he had no thought of comfort.

"Feel in my hip pocket; I think he left the key of these handcuffs."

They unlocked the irons and took them off, and he rubbed his bruised wrists.

"Have you found his car?"

Binny's saloon had not been located. The last time Surefoot had seen it, it was at the door of the cottage, but evidently, during one of his absences, the man had taken it to a hiding place. There was a small garage attached to the cottage – a tiny shed – but this was unoccupied.

By the light of the burning house they picked up the tracks. They crossed the grassland to the left of the cottage and must have passed over the very place where Binny had dug the grave. Thereafter they were difficult to trace, but obviously they went straight across the field in the same direction as the man had taken. A quarter of an hour later they picked up unmistakable evidence that the car had been left standing near a small secondary road. The gate was wide open and the tracks of the machine were visible on the soft, wet earth. He had not made for the main road again, but had turned up to the road to Cookham, where traffic would be practically non-existent at this hour of the night and the chances of observation nil.

The solitary police officer on duty at Cookham had seen the car pass, but had not observed the driver. He had turned on to the toll bridge, but at this hour of the night the toll gate is left open. The Bourne End police had seen several cars without taking particular notice of them. He could have taken the Oxford Road across the railway crossing, or he could have followed the river to Marlow.

Surefoot Smith rejected the suggestion that he should go home and rest, leaving the chase to the Flying Squad and the Buckinghamshire police; he rejected it violently and with oaths.

"This fellow can't go far, dressed as he is," he said, "in a singlet and trousers – I pulled most of his shirt off. He is going to hold up somebody, or burgle a house and get a new outfit. You realise what this man is, don't you? He is trained in the gang methods. He will not stop at murder – you are not dealing with an ordinary English criminal."

They were not kept waiting long for proof of this. Deciding upon the Marlow road as being more likely to offer opportunities for this desperado, they came upon a policeman pushing a bicycle. It was raining heavily, and his helmet and cape were dripping wet.

"A blue car passed here five minutes ago," he said.

The police car sped on. Just outside of Marlow they found the machine they were seeking; it was empty.

At three o'clock in the morning a car passing along the Oxford Road was stopped by a policeman, who stood in the middle of the roadway with outstretched arms. Driving the car was a well-to-do farmer from Oxford. He was inclined to be truculent at this stop.

"I am sorry to bother you," said the police officer, "but we are searching for an escaped murderer, and I want you to give me a lift to the other side of High Wycombe."

The farmer, rather intrigued, was not at all displeased, probably a little thrilled, to find himself a participant in a man hunt, and the policeman got into the uncomfortable rear seat of the car. It sped on through the Wycombes.

"I will tell you where to drop me," said the officer.

On the other side of High Wycombe there is a fork road which leads to Princes Risborough.

"Turn here," said the officer.

The driver expostulated – he had to get back to Oxford.

"Turn here," said the police officer, and something cold touched the nape of the farmer's neck.

"Do as you're told."

The policeman's voice was peremptory. The gun in his grimy hand was eloquent. The farmer almost jumped out of his seat with astonishment. He was not wanting in courage, but he was unarmed.

"What's your game?" he asked. He was still unsuspicious that the man behind him was anything but a policeman. "You're not allowed to do that sort of thing."

"Get it out of your nut that I'm a copper," said Binny. "The man whose clothes I'm wearing is lying in a ditch with a break in his bean. Drive where I tell you and save a lot of argument."

The driver turned the car in the direction indicated. They went along a new road, a portion of which was under construction. There were red lamps and a watchman's fire. Dimly the farmer realised that the man behind him was the wanted murderer, and the realisation chilled him.

They were in a country which even at high noon is a little deserted. It was a silent desert now. All the time Binny was watching left and right for a suitable place for his purpose. Presently they passed by the side of the road a wooden building that had the appearance of a barn, and he ordered the driver to stop and turn back. There was an open gate by the side of the barn, and through this they drove.

"Stop here," said Binny. He pushed open the door of the saloon. "Now get down."

He took the little electric lantern which had been part of the unfortunate policeman's equipment, and flashed it on to the door of the barn. It was unsecured by lock or hasp. He pulled open the door with one hand, covering his prisoner with the other.

"Go inside," he said, and followed.

Half an hour later he came out again, wearing the farmer's tweed suit and his high-collared waterproof jacket. He listened for a second at the door before closing it, got into the limousine, and backed on to the road. There was still a considerable danger of his being stopped. A solitary man driving a car would be suspect, no matter whose clothes he was wearing, and the present solution to his difficulty was merely a temporary measure.

If he could find one of those night trucks that run between London and the provinces it would serve him better. These express lorries carried two and often three men. He had to trust to luck.

Detection was certain if he took a direction which led him away from London. In the few hours that remained before the dawn he must work his way back to London. He had three bolt-holes; had the police found them all?

He drove through Aylesbury and worked right. He had an extraordinary knowledge of topography, and was aiming to reach the Great North Road and approach London from that direction.

Passing through a village, a policeman came out of the shadows and held up his hand. For a second Binny hesitated; his first impulse was to drive on, but he was none too certain of the immediate locality, and the chances were that if he did not stop now he would find a "barrage" a few miles farther on.

Binny had studied the police situation very carefully. He knew that the police could close London in a ring by the establishment of these barrage posts, and that he would be liable at any moment to come upon a place where a lorry was drawn up across the road. He knew too of the canvas belts, heavily spiked, which are thrown across the roadway, with disastrous consequences to the non-stop motorist.

He took his foot off the accelerator and brought his car to a standstill.

"Let me see your driving licence," said the police officer.

Binny stiffened. He had relieved his victim of all his portable goods, but a driving licence was not amongst them. Motorists have a trick of carrying this important document in the pocket attached to the door. If it were not there…

He slipped his gun out of his pocket and laid it on the seat by his side before he lifted up the flap of the pocket and began a search. His heart jumped as his fingers touched the familiar shape of the licence. He handed it out and the policeman examined it by the light of his lantern.

"Is this Dornby or Domby?" asked the officer.

"Dornby," said Binny promptly.

It was as likely to be that as the other. The officer handed back the licence without a word.

"You haven't seen anybody driving a blue saloon, have you – a man dressed in shirt and trousers?"

Binny chuckled.

"Well, I wouldn't be able to tell the colour of the saloon, and I certainly wouldn't see what the driver was wearing. Why? Do you want somebody?"

"There's been a murder committed," said the policeman vaguely. "We only had a vague idea as to why the 'arrest and detain' notice should have been issued. Goodnight, Mr Dornby."

Binny drove on. The policeman had not looked into that yellow face, but the next policeman might. They were pretty slick at Scotland Yard, he decided, and wondered how these isolated police posts should have been notified.

He looked at the licence. John Henry Domby was the name, of Wellfield Farm. He memorised this, put the licence in his pocket, and went on.

He had now reached a point where he could avoid villages, for he would soon be striking the North Road, where most efficient barrages would be established, especially when he reached the Metropolitan Police area.

He came at last to the long, winding road that runs from London through Doncaster to the north. Left or right? That was the problem.

He debouched on to the highway through a narrow lane with high banks. It was near a turn of the road. He heard the whir of a motor-car, saw the glow of headlamps, and turned sharply to the left.

The car that came round the corner was hugging the left of the road. The driver saw Binny's machine almost too late to avoid a collision. He swerved to the right, the car skidded on the slippery road, turned completely round, and, striking a telegraph post with one of its wheels, hung drunkenly over the side of the ditch.

Binny pulled up to avoid a second collision, for the wrecked machine was now immediately in front of him, and only by jamming on his brakes did he bring his own car to a standstill a few inches from the other. He heard the chauffeur shout, the door was jerked open, and a woman scrambled out into the glare of the headlamps.

Binny stared, hardly able to believe his eyes. The woman standing in the downpour was Mary Lane!

30

Security can be very irksome, especially when it is wedded to a lumpy bed in an ill-ventilated room. The sergeant's wife had given her the second best bedroom, which was, by most standards, a comfortable apartment. Mary felt desperately tired when she put out the light, but the moment her head touched the pillow all her weariness and desire for sleep had left her. She lay for half an hour, counting sheep, making up shopping lists, weaving stories, but grew wider and wider awake. At the end of that time she got up, turned on the light, and slipped into her dressing-gown.

She thought the mere act of rising would make her sleepy, but she had been mistaken. She was seized with a longing for her own comfortable quarters at the hotel, and began to dress. She could easily make an excuse to the sergeant's wife, who had gone out for the evening and would not be back till after midnight. There was no telephone in the quarters, but Surefoot Smith had made her free of the station, and she knew she had only to go downstairs and see the night inspector and he would put her in touch with the detective.

She felt horribly ungrateful, but, so far as she had been concerned, she had come to this safe retreat without any enthusiasm. The danger from Binny was probably exaggerated – Surefoot himself had told her that the man could have no further interest in her now that the hue and cry was out.

Scribbling a note to her hostess – a note which contained more lame excuses for her eccentricity than were necessary – she put on her coat and went down to the charge room.

The inspector to whom she had been introduced had gone out, visiting the patrols. Evidently he had not impressed upon the sergeant in charge the necessity for keeping a watchful eye upon the visitor, and he received her explanation for her return to the hotel with polite interest, until she mentioned the name of Surefoot Smith. Then he became very attentive.

"He's not at the Yard, miss. As a matter of fact, there's been some trouble there. We've had a special warning to look out for him."

She opened her eyes in astonishment.

"Look out for him?" And then, quickly: "Has he disappeared?"

The sergeant did not forget that reticence is the first duty of a constable, and became evasive.

"Is it something to do with Binny?" she insisted.

"Well, yes." He hesitated before he became more communicative. "He's the man wanted for the murder of the old man in Regent's Park. Yes, they've got an idea at the Yard that Binny's got him away somewhere. Rather a queer idea that a murderer can get away an inspector of the CID, but there you are!"

She sensed, without realising, the eternal if gentle rivalry between the uniformed and the ununiformed branches of the Metropolitan Police.

"How could an inspector be lured away? It sounds silly, doesn't it? Personally, I believe it's all bunk, but there you are! We're on the lookout for both of them."

She asked him to get her a cab, and again he was reluctant. Sergeants in charge of station houses have no time to find cabs for visitors; but she was evidently a friend of Surefoot Smith's and he stretched a point in her favour, telephoned to a cab rank, and five minutes later she was driving through the rain to Scotland Yard.

She left just as the squad cars were starting out in search of Surefoot, and she interviewed the Chief Inspector. He offered her very little information and a great deal of fatherly advice about going to bed. He evidently knew nothing whatever of Surefoot's plan to protect her, and was a little embarrassed when she asked if she might stay at Scotland Yard until some news was received.

"I shouldn't worry if I were you, Miss Lane," he said. "We've got police barrages on all the roads for thirty miles round London, and I am very certain that Surefoot will turn up. He's an erratic sort of individual, and I wouldn't be surprised to see him walk in at any moment."

Nevertheless, she was determined to stay, and he had her taken to Surefoot's own room.

It was a quiet room, and now that the first excitement of the night was over she realised how tired she was and how foolish she had been to leave even an uncomfortable bed.

She sat at the table, resting her head on one palm, found herself nodding, and, after a while, passing into that uneasy stage of semi-consciousness which is nearly sleep.

She woke with a jump as the Chief Inspector came in.

"Young lady, you go home," he said. "We've found Surefoot; so far as I can make out, he's not very badly hurt."

He told her briefly what had happened.

"Binny has escaped. Surefoot's theory is that he's breaking north. Have you ever noticed that a fugitive from justice invariably turns north? It's a fact – at least, nearly a fact. Now you go home, Miss Lane, and I'll send an officer round to your hotel in the morning with the latest news."

"Is he coming back to London?" she asked. "Mr Smith, I mean?"

The Chief smiled.

"If he had half the intelligence he's supposed to have he'd get himself admitted to a nursing home. No. We've formed a sort of headquarters barrage this side of Welwyn. Chief Inspector Roose is in charge, and Surefoot is going across for a consultation. He's all right – your friend Mr Allenby is with him."

He had a cab called and she drove to her hotel. She must have been half asleep for two hours, she saw as she passed Big Ben and heard two o'clock strike. She was wider awake than she had been at any period of the night.

The hall porter who admitted her was searching for her letters when she stopped him.

"Is there a place where I can hire a car?" she asked.

He looked at her in astonishment.

"Yes, miss. Do you want one tonight?"

She hesitated. The Chief had said that Dick and Surefoot were at Welwyn, but he had not said where. At first she supposed that they had taken up their quarters at the local police station – she was rather hazy as to what a barrage meant. But there would be policemen on the road, stopping cars, and they would direct her to where the two men could be found.

Why she should go at all was not quite clear even to herself. It was a desire to be "in it," to be close to the big events which touched her own life so closely, to see with her own eyes the development of the story in which she had been a character. She could find plenty of excuses; none that she could have stated convincingly.

"Yes, get me a car. Tell them to come round as soon as they can."

He gave her the key of her room and she went upstairs, and presently the porter came up after her, bringing some coffee he had made, for by night he was not only custodian but cook.

Leo Moran had been removed to his own flat, he told her, but mainly he talked, with a certain amount of pride, about the reporters who had been "coming and going" since the discovery of the gassed banker.

She had hardly finished her coffee before the car came, and, dressing herself a little more warmly, she went down and gave the driver instructions.

As the car drew out of the suburbs into the open country, Binny and his flight assumed a new significance. She was not sorry for him. If she was a little frightened, it was not of the man, but at the thought of the vast machinery that her brain had put into motion. The moment she had heard of that scrawled note on the back of the cheque she had solved the mystery of Binny's defalcations, and when she had heard that all the forgeries were dated the seventeenth of the month – the day that the old man invariably paid his tradesmen's bills – she was sure.

And now, because she had remembered the shape and appearance of the key of a kitchen door, because she had added cheques to key, eighteen thousand London policemen were looking for this bald-headed man. That was the frightening thing; not Binny and the menace of him, but the spectacle of these great winding wheels moving to crush a malefactor.

To Mary Lane, Binny was hardly as much an individual as a force. She thought the car was speeding a little dangerously on the wet road. Once she distinctly felt a skid, and gripped the arm-rest tightly.

They could not have been more than a few miles from Welwyn when, rounding a turn, she saw a car come into the road ahead, and went cold, for she realised that, at the speed they were travelling, it was almost impossible to avoid it. Her car swerved and turned giddily; she felt a crash, and was thrown violently to her knees as the machine canted over.

She reached up at the door, and by sheer physical strength flung it open and scrambled out on to the wet road. The chauffeur was already standing by the bonnet, staring at the car stupidly.

"I'm very sorry, miss," he said huskily. "I'll have to telephone for another car from town. Perhaps this gentleman will take you into Welwyn."

The second car, in avoiding which the accident had occurred, was behind them. Mary walked towards it as the driver got down from his seat. His coat collar was turned up, and she could not see his face.

"Had an accident?" he asked gruffly.

The chauffeur came forward.

"Will you drive us into Welwyn?" he asked. "I've smashed my near side front wheel."

"You'd better wait with the car. I'll drive the lady; it's only a couple of miles ahead," said the other. "Go on, miss, jump in; I'll drop you in the town and send back a breakdown gang for the car."

This arrangement apparently suited the chauffeur, and Mary followed the motorist, and, when he opened the door of his car, entered without any misgivings. He walked round the back of the machine, got in by the other door, and sat by her side. She could not see his face; his collar was still turned up. As he started the engine and moved on she thought she heard him laugh, and wondered what there was amusing in the situation.

"It's very good of you to take me," she said. "I'm afraid the accident was our fault."

He did not reply for a moment, but at last: "Accidents will happen," he said sententiously.

They went two or three hundred yards along the road, and then suddenly the car turned left. She knew roughly the position of Welwyn, knew enough at any rate to realise that they were going away from the town.

"Haven't you made a mistake?" she asked.

"No." His reply was short and gruff, but it aroused in her no more than a sense of resentment.

From the second road they turned into a third, a narrow lane which ran roughly parallel with the main road. It skirted some big estate; high trees banked up one side of the lane, and a wire fence cut the estate from the road. The car slowed, and as they came abreast of a white gate, stopped. The driver turned the machine so that the headlamps searched the gate and revealed its flimsy character. Without hesitation he sent the car jerking forward, crashing one of the lamps and sending the gate into splinters.

Beyond was a fairly smooth gravel road, and up this the car sped.

"Where are we going?"

A cold chill was at the girl's heart; an understanding of her danger set her trembling from head to foot.

Binny did not reply till they had gone a hundred yards. He found an opening between the trees on the right, set the car in that direction, and jolted on for another fifty yards. Then he stopped the machine.

"What is the meaning of this?" she asked.

"You're a very nice young lady, a very sweet young lady. Charmed to meet you again in such romantic circumstances."

As she heard that mincing, affected voice she almost swooned. Binny! The horror of her discovery came to her with full force, as he went on: "Friend of Mr Allenby's – fiancée, aren't you, young lady? And a friend of my dear friend, Surefoot Smith."

She reached out for the door handle and tried to rise, but he threw her back.

"I've had several ideas about you. The first was that nobody would stop me if they saw me driving with a lady. Then it struck me that I was being optimistic. The second thought that occurred to me, my dear, was that you might be of great assistance to me. And the third thought, my sweet young thing, was that, if the worst came to the worst – they can only hang you once, you know, whatever you do. Not that they will hang me," he went on quickly, "I am too clever for them. Now we'll get out and see where we are."

He leaned over her, pushed open the door, and, catching her by the arm, guided her to the ground.

Just before she had left the hotel the porter had handed her a thick bundle of letters. She had advertised for a maid and had given the hotel as her address; these were some of the replies. She had thrust them into her pocket, and as she stepped from the car she remembered them. She drew one from her pocket and dropped it on the ground.

Binny had retained the lantern he had taken from the policeman, and with the aid of this they found their way through the plantation.

"You and I will find another car."

He chatted pleasantly, and even in her terror she could find time to wonder how he could return to the character of Washington Wirth. It was grotesque, unbelievable, like a bad dream.

"I am a man of infinite resource," he went on, never releasing his grip of her arm. "For hundreds of years they will talk about Binny, just as today they talk about Jack Sheppard. And the wonderful thing about it is that I shall end my life quietly, as a respectable member of society. Possibly be a town councillor or a mayor in a colonial town – a pleasing prospect and a part that I could act!"

It was at this point she dropped her third letter. She must husband her trail; the supply of letters was not inexhaustible. She dropped her fourth as they started to cross the corner of a field.

All the time he kept up his incessant babble.

"You need have no qualms, my dear young lady. No harm will come to you – for the moment. Whilst you are alive, I am alive! You are a hostage – that is the word, isn't it?"

She made no reply. The first feeling of panic had worn off. She could only speculate upon what would happen at the last, when this desperate man was in a corner and she was at his mercy.

Before them loomed against the night sky the outlines of a big house. They came to a lawn surrounded by an iron fence, and, walking parallel with this, they reached on open gateway and a paved yard.

Once or twice there had been a lull in his monologue. He had stopped to listen. It was a very still night; the sound of distant rumbling trains, the whine of motor-cars passing along the highway came to them distinctly. He was apparently satisfied, for he made no comment. Now, as they passed into a tiled yard, he stopped again and listened, turning his head backwards. As he did so he saw the flash of a lamp – only for the fraction of a second, and then it disappeared. It seemed to come from the plantation they had left. He had left his lights burning – was that it? He moved left and right a few paces, and did not see the light again.

The possibility that there were gamekeepers in the wood now occurred to him. It was obviously a covert of some kind; the lower part of the fence was made of wire netting.

He never once released his hold of the girl. She felt the tenseness of the moment and held her breath. Then, without a word, he guided her into the yard, and now she observed that he used his lamp with greater caution. There were stables here; two of the half doors were wide open and hung on broken hinges. There was no need to make any further investigation; the house to which the stables were attached was unoccupied.

They came to what was evidently a kitchen door and found a small, weather-stained notice.

"Keys at Messrs. Thurlow, Welwyn."

There was a long casement window at the back of the house. Binny pushed the barrel of his pistol through two panes, groped for the catch, and, finding it, pulled it open.

"Get in – " he began, and at that moment he was caught in a circle of blinding light.

From somewhere in the yard a powerful lamp was turned on him, and a voice he hated said: "Don't move, Binny!"

It was Surefoot Smith.

For a second he stood, paralysed, his arm still clasping the girl's. Suddenly he jerked her before him, his arm round her waist.

"If you come anywhere near me I'll shoot," he said, and she felt the cold barrel of a gun glide along her neck.

"What's the good of being silly, Binny?" Surefoot's voice was almost caressing.

They could not see him in the glare of the light that he or somebody held.

"Stand your trial like a man. It's fifty-fifty we've got nothing on you."

"You haven't, eh?" snarled Binny. "That dog doesn't fight, Smith. You take your men and clear them out of this place. Give me an hour, and I'll leave this baby without hurting her. Come any closer and I'll blow her head off – and then you'll have something on me. It won't be fifty-fifty either."

There was a long pause, and the girl heard the low voices of men in conversation.

"All right," said Surefoot at last. "I'll give you an hour, but you'll hand over the girl right away."

Binny laughed harshly.

"Am I a child? I'll leave her when I'm safe. You go back to where you came, and – "

That was all he said. The silent-footed man who had worked round behind him struck swiftly with a rubber truncheon. The girl had only time to swing herself clear before he crumpled and fell.

The chauffeur of the wrecked car had been in luck. Hardly had Binny disappeared before another machine came into the sight, and the chauffeur begged a lift into Welwyn. Less than a mile along the road they ran into a police barrage and he told his story. He gave valuable information, for he had seen the lights of Binny's car turn from the road.

"Practically you were never out of sight, from the moment you left the plantation," said Surefoot. "The broken gate gave him away, and he left the lights of his car burning. It was easy, even without the trail of letters you left. Very scientific, but we didn't see them!"

The arrest and conviction of Binny had a demoralising effect upon Surefoot Smith. On the day this wholesale murderer stood on the trap in Pentonville Prison, Surefoot departed from the rule of a lifetime, refused all beer and drank spirits. As he explained to Dick Allenby: "If ever there was a day to get soused – that was the day!"

EDGAR WALLACE

THE JOKER
(USA: THE COLOSSUS)

While the millionaire Stratford Harlow is in Princetown, not only does he meet with his lawyer Mr Ellenbury but he gets his first glimpse of the beautiful Aileen Rivers, niece of the actor and convicted felon Arthur Ingle. When Aileen is involved in a car accident on the Thames Embankment, the driver is James Carlton of Scotland Yard. Later that evening Carlton gets a call. It is Aileen. She needs help.

THE SQUARE EMERALD
(USA: THE GIRL FROM SCOTLAND YARD)

'Suicide on the left,' says Chief Inspector Coldwell pleasantly, as he and Leslie Maughan stride along the Thames Embankment during a brutally cold night. A gaunt figure is sprawled across the parapet. But Coldwell soon discovers that Peter Dawlish, fresh out of prison for forgery, is not considering suicide but murder. Coldwell suspects Druze as the intended victim. Maughan disagrees. If Druze dies, she says, 'It will be because he does not love children!'